THE BRIAR AND THE BLIGHT

JB TREPAGNIER

The Briar and the Blight

It wasn't worth the hassle of anyone finding out my secret

Guttertown is the filthy underbelly of Nestran. Everyone knows everyone's secrets, but they don't know mine.

Being the bastard daughter of *the* most powerful Baron in Nestran won't end well for me. They've managed to keep kings and queens who can set things on fire with their minds under their control since the war. Like, I have much of a chance against them if I ever announced myself as his daughter and asked for help.

Which is why my mother raised me as a boy. Even *I* thought I was a boy until my period started at ten and I thought I was dying. She told me why she lied. If I *ever* needed help from my father, he was going to require me to pay him back by working at the brothels.

I've kept up the ruse, but it's a lot more complicated now. I had four best friends when I thought I was a boy. I'm still close with them, but I'm desperately in love with three of them and the fourth is now my mortal enemy. Not like I can do much about any of that except keep hating Neco.

Except my mom has a cough and my father would have the best healers if it's serious. She'd forbid me from asking, but she's my world.

If I have to play his soldier, I will. I'm just not thinking

about what will happen if he finds out I'm his daughter, not his son.

Idric Island
Inanos
Farrhi
Tark
NESTRAN

N
GUTTERTOWN

NECO

I stepped over the growing puddle of blood. Slitting throats was intimate, but very messy. They could match my boot print if I tracked blood. I didn't need it on me because I wasn't even supposed to be in the Trulos District. This was the merchants' district, and they didn't take too kindly to Guttertown trash here.

I didn't take kindly to rich merchants coming to a Guttertown brothel and beating the shit out of one of the girls, hence why I broke into his house and slit his throat.

Nestran law didn't care about men who hurt women and children. They cared less if those women and children lived in Guttertown. That kind of behavior couldn't be corrected. They wouldn't get it if I also beat the shit out of them. They'd get all whiney about it and have me thrown in the cells.

But slitting their throats? I was doing *everyone* a favor, and I was so good at it, they never laid eyes on me. I wasn't a stupid vigilante serial killer. I didn't sit them down and explain to them *why* I was killing them. Fuck that.

It wasn't that I was worried about bonding with them or letting them go. I hated everyone except my momma and little sister. People were awful and all eventually let you down. I just didn't care to explain. No one told a roach why they were stepping on it. The people I killed were all roaches.

I looked through his things. I wasn't going to steal anything that could be traced back to me, but his type always had a bag of coins hidden somewhere. It wouldn't be super obvious if I took it and once I burned the bag it was in, it wouldn't trace me back to the crime scene.

The money would find its way to the person they hurt. If there was more than one bag, and there usually was, then my momma and sister got new dresses and we ate well for a little while.

In the richer parts of Nestran, you could go to the market and buy the best cuts of meat if you had enough coin. Guttertown was dirt poor and our market was less extensive.

Our hunting grounds were also limited. We weren't supposed to hunt outside the borders of Guttertown and the shifters had villages around here we couldn't go near because of the war. They'd kill us on sight. They probably should. We did terrible shit to their kind.

Yes! This idiot had three bags of gold and silver stashed in a book he'd hollowed out. I needed to get out of here before his wife woke up. I'd divide it into two bags. My family and the woman he hurt would do pretty well with this for months.

My momma was getting a cough. I could buy medicine. Hopefully, I could get it better before I had to contact my father. All the Argent kids in Guttertown were bastards. We couldn't take our mother's family name for stupid-ass reasons and our fathers would have to give us theirs. We all had different fathers, but we all had the last name Argent.

If you didn't know who your daddy was, it was one of the Barons, the rich fucks running things. Guttertown men always claimed their sons, even if they were had out of wedlock. The Barons only did if they could profit off of them.

I knew the fuck-bag who sired me because he came back ten years later and forced Momma to be his mistress again. Guttertown women didn't have a choice when a Baron set his eyes on her. He ruined her life even worse the second time he came around.

If I could kill him, I would, but he was too high profile.

For now, I needed to sneak through the Trulos District and through the areas of Nestran that Guttertown wasn't allowed, to get home. Which I did quite easily.

We lived in a brothel because my momma worked there. Pretty much all of us Argent kids lived at one because our mommas needed to feed us and this was the only way. I didn't have a problem with sex work, but I wanted my momma to be able to retire and just eat cake.

She was coming out of the bathroom when I got home.

"Neco? You know I hate it when you're out late."

Yeah, she did. It would break her heart if she knew I was slitting throats, too, but someone needed to protect these women and kids in a way that it never traced back to Guttertown.

Don't ask me where I got my size. My momma was barely five feet tall and after I hit my growth spurt, I shot up six inches taller than my sperm donor and filled out. I had to lean down to kiss her on the head. My sister was going to be small like my mom. Thankfully, we both looked like our mother. I had a long scar on over the eye I was missing, but even with the scar and eye patch, it would probably make me even more homicidal to see that dick's face in the mirror every time I shaved.

"I was taking care of a job. I'm going to go hunting in the morning. Use this to get new dresses and give Rowena a proper name day. Maybe show her how to alter dresses and cook again so I can figure out where to get her an apprenticeship."

Most people apprenticed with their family, but some

people didn't have enough kids and would take people on to employ. I wanted Rowena to have a *choice*.

Some women worked at the brothel because life shat on them and they didn't have any other options. Some were enterprising women who decided if men were willing to pay for it, they were happy to take their coins. My momma had been shat on because of my sperm donor, but I'd be damned if Rowena was forced into anything she didn't want.

I taught her to beat up all the boys by the time she was five. I couldn't always watch her and I didn't hurt kids. Best teach her to fight her own battles. I wanted the best for my baby sister and since our father hadn't exactly stepped up and left us in a shitty situation, it was up to me to provide.

"She's still going through her phase where she only wants to be a soldier. She beat the shit out of Seff again."

Which wasn't how any of that worked. The Barons waited until their kids were desperate and came to them for help. I was a big guy, so he'd want me for his army. It was different for the girls and I was *never* letting things get to that point.

I grunted.

"If Seff hadn't started shit the first time, she wouldn't have fought back. He keeps going after her to save face that a tiny ten-year-old girl whooped his arse, and she keeps doing it again. Twelve-year-old boys are stupid as fuck. One day, she'll pop him in the face hard enough that it sinks in."

Momma sighed.

"You shouldn't encourage her to settle everything with her fists. In two years, she's going to finish school and have to pick a trade. She'll have to learn to play nice if she wants to keep it."

I just grunted. Guttertown schools weren't fancy, like the rest of Nestran. We didn't have fancy tutors or university. We went long enough to learn to read and write so we could sign our names to contracts and read it well enough that we didn't get fucked over.

We learned math enough to count money and run a business. The only history we got was a basic overview of the war when humans first came to Nestran and fought the shifters. I might have only gotten a basic education, but something told me there was a *lot* more to that story and the tribes of shifters had a totally different version of that war.

"Rowena will find her way. Get some sleep. I'll be gone when you both wake up. I'm going to get a wild boar for Rowena's name day. I'm feeling lucky."

"Get some rest, too. I worry about you sometimes, Neco."

My momma walked away coughing. She'd developed this cough over the past few days. It could just be minor or it could be something that needed a healer. I hoped it wasn't something that needed a better healer than Guttertown had or I'd have to contact my father. He'd use me and I'd have to manage to do that without him using Rowena, too.

I'd pick some Elderberries while I was hunting. That should help Momma if this was minor. Because I definitely never wanted to lay eyes on my father again.

LUCY

I woke up and stretched. I lived above a tavern, so I could sleep with my window open and not worry about perverts or cats sneaking in. I *shouldn't* have to worry about perverts since everyone thought I was a boy, but this was Guttertown. The rest of Nestran took offense at same-sex relationships, but Guttertown certainly didn't. I made a very pretty boy, if I did say so myself. It could be a male or female pervert with consent issues that snuck in my window. This *was* Guttertown.

I stood at the window. Not right at it because people could see me in my nightshirt, but far enough to breathe in the fresh air. Guttertown smelled like mangoes with the faint undercurrent of urine. Sometimes, you could catch a pleasant breeze where it was mostly mangoes and hardly any urine. There was a copse of mango trees just outside my window, so I got lucky a lot.

Yeah, there were all kinds of urban legends about why we had an overabundance of mangoes. We stole this land from the shifters after the war. This was the site of the mass grave during the war when they killed the Tempris.

The shifters were all elementals. They shifted into Earth, Air, or Water animals, and then you had the Tempris. They didn't shift, but they controlled fire. We thought they were the most dangerous during the war and killed most of them. Our ancestors left two of them alive to rule to keep the tribes in line, but we'd been trying to breed them out of existence since.

They were only allowed to have one child, and they had to marry a human. Guttertown wasn't exactly allowed near the palace, but I was told the current king and his daughter didn't even have the signature red hair and violet eyes anymore.

I'm pretty sure the Barons got tired of waiting because the Princess Esylle's daughter got kidnapped out of thin air when I was about five years old. I didn't remember much about it, but nowadays, everyone thought the Princess Lisana was dead and the Tempris line would die with her.

But first things first. I stepped away from my window. I needed to bind my chest. For the first ten years of my life, I actually thought I was a boy named Lance. I'd never seen a naked boy before to know I was different. Then, I hit ten and started my period. Man, was that a mind fuck! I thought I was dying.

Thankfully, it happened when I was at home and I could run to my mom. I loved the shit out of my mom. She was all I had. You pretty much knew if you didn't have a dad in Guttertown and your mom wasn't telling you stories about how he died, then your dad was a Baron. Most everyone was super careful with herbs unless they were being lied to by a stupid sack of shit about how he was going to take care of you.

I'd always known my father was a Baron, but the day I woke up with blood on my sheets was when I found out I definitely wasn't a boy and why my mom disguised me. Sometimes, the bastards of Guttertown would need financial help from their Baron fathers. They were always willing to help, but there was a cost.

They wanted our bodies.

The men got put to work, either as a soldier or guard and the women? It was one thing to work at the brothels because you wanted to or because you landed on shit times. You paid the Madame her cut, and you kept the rest. If you were the daughter of a Baron? The Madame got her cut, the Baron got his cut, and you got the rest. And it was hardly enough to live on unless you never slept or got off your back.

Mom didn't want that for me. She knew I might eventually have to ask my father for help. I was furious about it because my entire life was a lie. That was until she told me who my father was. I might have only been ten, but I knew who Folcard was.

The Tempris king ruled in name only and the Barons ran roughshod all over him, but it was Folcard who really ran the show. He was the *worst* out of all the Barons. If there was an unfair tax, it was usually his idea. If someone got shafted in a deal, it was Folcard. If someone disappeared? Also Folcard.

Yeah, I got over my shit and agreed to keep up the ruse.

Mom said my name was actually Lucy, not Lance, and taught me how to pretend. I'd learned most of it actually thinking I was a boy, but puberty made it loads harder. For one thing, I grew tits. They weren't massive, but they were a nice size. When I had to start strapping them down with bandages, I couldn't even appreciate them.

And no one prepares you for how gross teenage boys are. Or how gross you'll have to pretend to be to fit in. Honestly, sometimes, I wanted to punch them in the fucking face instead of laughing at what they were saying. They eventually grew out of that for the most part and were mostly tolerable now.

Binding my chest sucked, and I always wondered what I would look like with long hair. I had to use bandages because I couldn't exactly buy anything at the market or seamstress. I had permanent scars from binding my chest, and it was always such a relief to take the bindings off at night.

I just ignored the total mind fuck that I spent the first ten years of my life thinking I was a boy and was still living as one.

Once I had myself presentable as I boy, I went into the kitchen, where my mom was making breakfast. She was one of the few women who had taken up with a Baron and didn't get completely ruined.

That would be because if we didn't live in Guttertown, Mom would have been an alchemist. She didn't completely fall for Folcard's crap. She'd been studying and socking away money. The tavern we lived above was ours. Mom could have been a healer, but she learned to brew ale and make whiskey.

We'd done pretty decent for ourselves, but we had overhead, employees, and taxes to pay. And Mom had been coughing, so we were going to need a healer soon. Mom taught me everything she knew, and I had a concoction going in the basement that should earn us a pretty penny if I ever got it right.

I was trying to make an entirely new spirit that could be made with grains or potatoes and then I was going to infuse it with all the mangoes we had lying around. I just needed to perfect it first, and I wasn't there yet. I was about to go check on my experiments when Mom stopped me.

"Sit and eat. It'll be there after and I'm not having you get scrawny when you're friends with all those boys."

One thing about my mom. When she had that look on her face, you did what she said. She knew me better than anyone alive and she knew damned well I was going to skip breakfast, tinker in the basement, and then probably forget lunch unless she dragged me out.

She was paler than I would have liked and she hunched over the stove for a few minutes to cough. Fuck my experiments. My mom was my world. She was the most important person to me in all of Nestran.

"Nope. You're taking today off. Ollie and me will run the tavern."

"Are you going to be nice to him?" Mom asked with a smile.

Ugh. Mom knew damned well I was in love with Ollie. We grew up together because his parents used to own this tavern. They did Mom a solid, hiring her to make their spirits. They both died unexpectedly and Mom was able to buy the tavern. Ollie was taken in by his uncle and my mom set the expectation that she would hire Ollie when he came of age and eventually, we'd be co-owners.

Which was actually perfect because Mom knew damned well, I wanted to be in the basement experimenting with making new spirits rather than actually running a tavern and Ollie loved everyone and everyone loved Ollie. He was perfect for being the face of the house.

Ollie flirted with me, even though he thought I was a boy, but he could also bat those big green eyes and use that silver tongue to get our stubborn donkey to do its thing when that fucking ass tried to kick me more than once.

And when he flirted with me, I got mad at him because it wasn't fair. I didn't think Ollie gave a shit either way if I was a boy or a girl. If I explained to him why I lied, he'd probably accept it since he was pretty easygoing. It was just that he had a big fucking mouth and I didn't need him blabbing my secret to the entire tavern.

"Probably not," I said.

"You could always *tell* him you're a girl."

I just grunted. Ten years as a boy and I could definitely grunt and go nonverbal.

"I mean it. Come down for food and to get something to drink, but you aren't working today," I fussed.

Mom just tipped her head at me. She was about to tell me something snarky, but then she started coughing. Mom and I had made several spirits that kept the tavern going, but I knew my experiment in the basement was going to take off if I could figure it out.

I just hoped that happened before her cough got worse.

OLIVER

I was able to open the tavern a little earlier today. Caitrin and Lance had been buying meat when needed because Lance was scrawny and had trouble carrying deer and boar home, but when my parents were running this place, my dad hunted. I had no problem hunting because Lance was usually needed in the basement figuring out drinks.

My uncle was also a farmer, so that helped. We had enough meat to serve stew tonight. I'd have to hunt again in the morning, but I was fine with that. When I unlocked the door, Lance was already getting things started. Which was weird because the arrangement we had was that Caitrin and I worked the front of the house most of the time unless Caitrin was helping Lance with alchemist shit brewing spirits.

"Mom's cough is worse. I told her to take the day off. I'll be helping."

Yeah, and being cranky pants about it, too. Did I mention I was madly in love with Lance? Lance had no right to be that beautiful. He had short, blond hair, but it had red highlights when the light hit it. His eyes were a lighter shade of blue than even the sky. I wanted to kiss that pouty mouth that was always insulting me. Lance had this lithe body.

Alas, after I hit my growth spurt, realized I was attracted to him, and started hitting on him, he made it clear he wasn't into other men. Which was a shame. We couldn't marry in the eyes of the king and Barons, but we could definitely get Guttertown married.

I was into the person, not the gender, but not everyone was like that. I backed off and never got sexual with Lance, but I did try to make him laugh and that seemed to piss him off, too. One day, that man was going to laugh at one of my jokes. Asking him to sling ale when his mind was on a basement project was going to be a disaster.

Lance could flirt and joke with the best of us, but he was happiest in the basement. And from what he told me, what he was working on could bring us a lot of money.

"Actually, Ronan was asking to sling ale or work in the kitchen for a few nights. One of the Barons commissioned him and then shafted him when it came time to pay him. He couldn't exactly refuse to hand it over until he got his money because the Baron would retaliate and he'd never get another commission again.

"We've had a few good nights and can afford to pay him. I don't like Caitrin's cough, either. It'll give her a few nights off and you the time to figure out your formula. Everyone loves Ronan and bitching about the Barons. They'll all show up to drink when they find out what they did to him. It benefits everyone. You get time to tinker with your formula, Caitrin gets to heal, and Ronan is a friend."

"Ugh. That Baron is shit for that. You know Mom would have let him work even if she wasn't sick and sales were bad, but everyone loves your stupid face and business has been booming since you were old enough to take over a little. Ronan is one of us."

I grinned.

"You're literally the *only* person in Nestran who thinks my face is stupid."

Because I was just as pretty as Lance, just in a very different way. Lance had this androgynous beauty, but I bulked up helping on my uncle's farm growing up. Beck was another one of our friends we grew up with, like Ronan. His mom was the Madame. He took his bodyguard duties seriously, but any time I visited him just to hang out, I got offered freebies.

Was that a blush? Did I just catch the unflappable Lance Argent blushing over something I just said? Was he maybe *slightly* into men and was just starting to realize it? I didn't get a chance to find out because Lance went stomping off towards the basement.

As soon as Lance left, Neco Argent flung the door open and stepped inside. Lance and Neco may or may not be related. No one would know until their mothers name dropped their fathers. Since they hadn't, it was one of the Barons. If it wasn't a Baron, a Guttertown woman would name and shame all day if he didn't step up.

Neco was a complete psychopath, but he was a friend. Case in point, he was covered in blood.

"That your blood or someone else's?"

Neco hated everyone but his mother and sister and he had no problem letting them know that. He tolerated me. One day, I was going to make the big brute my friend again. Because Neco Argent was sexy in the most dangerous way possible.

His mom avoided the brothels after he was born but got forced into it after she got pregnant with his sister. The Madame took them in, gave them a room, and let Theda choose when she wanted to start working.

Theda was passing through the lounge where the working girls were finding clients to get a bite to eat when she was just about to pop with Rowena. There wasn't a single woman who would have agreed to have sex that far along because it wasn't safe.

Some entitled merchant thought if he paid enough, Theda would do it. She refused and when he tried to make her the Madame ordered him to leave. He got violent, but her bodyguard was putting out a fire in one of the rooms, so ten-year-old Neco stepped in.

Neco got the shit kicked out of him, lost an eye, and had a long scar over that missing eye, but he took it personally. Neco just kind of exploded when he hit fifteen and grew to be this massive guy. He also got hot as fuck with that eye patch and scar.

I was also one hundred percent sure he was killing people.

Our tavern was right next door to the brothel and, as a barkeeper, I got all the gossip. If someone hurt one of those girls or a Guttertown brat, I heard about it. I also heard some tales about men getting their throats slit in the dead of night with no witnesses and no evidence. Beck told me the girl who got hurt always had a bag of money on her nightstand when she woke up like magic. It wasn't that hard to put two and two together.

Of course, I was never going to bring this up. Honestly, good for Neco. Those people shat on us and abused us and constantly got away with it. Still, I didn't think Neco was careless enough to walk around covered in blood. He just flung his black hair out of his eyes. Fuck me, he was hot.

"Well, it's certainly not mine, and I'm not about to get caught walking around with human blood on me. I caught a boar earlier this morning," he said, winking at me.

Interesting. Was Neco Argent into men? I'd hit that. I'll bet he'd hold you down and choke you, but he was a big cuddler afterwards. Still, if he wasn't, I wouldn't hint I was thinking about it. He seemed to have an MO with who he killed, but I definitely didn't want to be next.

"Most people wash after they clean their kills."

"No time. It's Rowena's name day and I've come into some funds to make it a good one. Can we use your uncle's land for the party? I could roast the boar there and Momma is going to bake a cake. You're all invited, of course. I think Rowena and your cousin have crushes on each other."

"Is that going to end badly for Baryn?"

Everyone adored Rowena. That kid had spunk. She punched me in the kidneys once and it fucking hurt for a pocket-sized Guttertown brat. Neco made sure *no one* was going to hurt that girl. Neco had his thing about hurting kids, but he might make an exception if his sister got hurt.

"Nah. I told Rowena not to start shit, but to finish it if someone else wants to. She's not going to hit him unless he hits her first."

"Um, your sister tried to make my kidneys bleed with her fist and I didn't do a fucking thing to her."

"That was just a misunderstanding," Neco said, waving his hand. "Anyway, can we have her party on your uncle's land?"

"Yeah. I don't even have to ask. Rowena is over all the time and she's bonded with one of the horses. She's got a way with animals. If you aren't careful, my uncle is going to steal her when she finishes school and teach her to break horses."

"Good. Right now, she wants to be a soldier."

That sounded accurate. Rowena would probably make a hell of a general. In Guttertown, the women could kick your ass just as well as the men, but in the rest of Nestran, women didn't and weren't allowed to fight.

"We'll make it happen. Tell my uncle I sent you, but if you open with it's for Rowena's name day, he's going to automatically say it's okay. Your sister is one of Guttertown's favorite brats."

"Thanks."

Neco let his mask slip for a minute. I think he honestly thought I was going to tell him no. Everyone really did love Rowena and as far as I was concerned, Neco was a hero fighting for the people the rest of Nestran shit on and the law wouldn't do anything about.

As a bartender, I heard a lot of secrets. I kept most of them. I only repeated what I overheard to the appropriate parties if someone was going to get hurt or shafted.

Neco kept to himself, but he could probably use a friend, even if he might not want a fuck buddy. I could be that friend by keeping an ear and eye out for him.

RONAN

Ollie, Lance, Beck, and I used to be inseparable when we were kids. Neco used to be a part of our group, but he pulled away after he lost his eye. We might have been eventually able to coax him back, but Lance went too hard trying to pull him back to the fold and Neco said some nasty things to him.

Then, Lance got his feelings hurt and when he saw some kids picking on Neco because of his eye and scar, he had a moment of weakness and said something cruel to Neco about his missing eye. Lance instantly regretted it and that wasn't Lance at all, but the damage was done. Lance ran after Neco to apologize and Neco broke his nose. They'd been mortal enemies ever since and Neco acted like the rest of us didn't exist except for Ollie. If you wanted decent food and strong alcohol, you kind of *had* to talk to Ollie. If Neco walked in and Lance was working front of house, he turned around and walked right back out.

I wished I could fix it, but there wasn't much I could do when Neco pretended I was invisible when I tried to talk to him. Beck, Ollie, and Lance? We were thick as thieves. They *always* had my back.

Guttertown didn't have much use for art. There wasn't much point in commissioning it when you could barely afford food or taxes. But it was my passion, and I was *good* at it. I didn't have any fancy art teachers or paints I bought from the market like the rest of Nestran artists. I was self-taught, and I made my paints from what I could forage in nature.

I could have apprenticed with the blacksmith, but I didn't want to. I didn't want to make horseshoes and shit to kill people with. I wanted to make *real* beauty. So, I skimped and took odd jobs while trying to get the people outside of Guttertown to buy my art.

It was slow going because they thought I was uncultured by default, but eventually, I started getting patrons. I wanted to be noticed, but not *too* noticed because you couldn't say no when the Barons commissioned you, but they never paid like they were entitled to my work for free.

Case in point. Ollie and Lance were lifesavers. I got to the tavern right when Neco was leaving.

"Hey, Neco."

He breezed right by me like I wasn't even here. I sighed. I missed Neco. I walked into the tavern as Ollie was cleaning glasses.

"Hey, working is no problem. Caitrin is sick, so we need the help, but you know we would have let you, anyway. I have a plan."

Ollie's plans got us into a lot of trouble when we were younger. I'd like to say Ollie grew out of that, but he didn't.

"We aren't going to spend a night in the cells, are we?"

"Not that kind of plan. Neco was in here because it's Rowena's name day. I'm not sure I can do anything about him and Lance because Lance fucked up and Neco doesn't want his apology, but I know how to fix it with you and Neco. He's civil with Beck because Beck protects the girls."

"Neco was stubborn long before he went no contact with us and frankly, he's a little scary now."

He really was, but in a kind of sexy way. He dressed in all black, his hair was black, his one eye was black, his skin was tanned, and he always had a five o'clock shadow. Neco also always had this look on his face, like he was five seconds away from gutting someone if they looked at him wrong.

"Neco is a teddy bear as long as you don't hurt women or children."

Ugh. Did Ollie get horny for everyone? Yes, Neco was hot, but I wouldn't describe him as a teddy bear *at all*. Neco had never been cuddly.

"I'm just going to trust you on that."

"No, listen. It's Rowena's name day. I like that kid. I'm pretty sure she's going to marry my cousin if he doesn't fuck it up or she grows up and her feelings change. My uncle already wants to adopt her and apprentice her to break his stallions. Neco came into some funds and he wants to throw her a party at the farm.

"I was thinking you could bring some parchment and charcoal and offer to do little sketches of the kids. Like, if one of them wants a sketch of them riding a dragon, you could do it. Rowena is probably going to want one of her standing on the corpses of her enemies. Guttertown kids *never* get that kind of thing. Consider it an extra shift. I'll pay you and it might get Neco talking to you again."

Yeah, fuck that. It was one thing when the Barons wanted my art for free. This was different.

"Listen, you only have to pay me for my shifts at the tavern. I don't care if Neco ignores me the entire time and doesn't decide to speak to me again. I know what it's like to be a Guttertown kid and wanting to be exposed to art or to see myself in the stories my mom told me. I can't think of a better place to do free art."

"Free art?" Lance said, coming up from the basement. "Why are you giving your art away for free?"

He must have just caught the tail end of that. None of us had any right to be this attracted to our best friend, but how dare Lance be that attractive? Ollie, Beck, and I had fooled around before and talked about how amazing it would be to bring Lance into it, but Lance was firmly into girls.

We all decided we were going to lose our virginity at the brothel when we were sixteen. We were all fumbling idiots who probably offended the hell out of the woman we were with, *except* Lance. Like, no one was smiling when we left our rooms except the woman who was fawning over Lance and telling him to come back any time.

Lance swore he'd been a virgin, too, but we all had our doubts. Everyone sucked their first time. No one knew what he had done to that woman since he refused to tell us, but every time we went back there to see Beck, she remembered him and wanted a repeat. Every single woman the rest of us were with that night managed to disappear when they saw us again.

All Lance would tell us was that if we were getting off, we needed to make damned sure the woman did, too. We saw her reaction to Lance, so we learned.

I guess it was safe to say if a virgin had spent that much time researching how to please a woman, they definitely weren't into men. Pity.

"I'm going to draw the kids at Rowena's name day. Neco had a windfall, and he's throwing her a party."

"Neat idea. It's a pity Neco is such an arse."

"Lance," Ollie said.

"What? The fucker broke my nose."

"And you said some hurtful shit before and after."

"Yeah, but I didn't get *violent*. That was uncalled for. I'll apologize for what I said when he apologizes for punching me in the face. Rowena is a good kid and I don't blame you for wanting to make her name day special. I'm going to get her a present, but I'm not going if he's going to be there."

Yeah, Neco and Lance in the same vicinity were going to be a bad idea. Neco just ignored me, but it tended to get explosive if those two couldn't avoid each other. Neco hadn't hit Lance again, but the shouting matches were usually epic.

"How's the experiment?"

"I think I've got a potent spirit, but it's nearly odorless and doesn't have a strong taste on its own like ale or whiskey. I've got the spirit down. It's good in a pinch if you want to get messy, but I'm trying to infuse it with all these fucking mangoes and herbs so it gets you fucked up and tastes good, too. It's not right yet," Lance grumbled.

He was probably going through things I didn't remotely understand in his head. Lance and Caitrin could have done anything involving alchemy if they weren't born in Guttertown. Fuck, if Lance's father had half a brain, he would have swooped Caitrin up and gotten her tutors. The woman was brilliant. If he'd bothered checking in on his son, he would have seen Lance was, too, and meant for better things than figuring out how to get Guttertown drunk.

"We've got this handled if you need to work."

"There's nothing left to do except let everything infuse."

"I have no idea what that means," Ollie said.

"This part is like cooking and figuring out a recipe. The spirit part is done and we could sell it as is. It's strong as fuck and will get them drunk. It's probably going to cause a hell of a hangover, so if we want them to buy it again, it needs to taste delicious. I'm tweaking the recipe."

Ollie and I both groaned. Caitrin was an amazing cook, and she made sure Lance would make a different kind of husband than the rest of Nestran. Lance was great in the kitchen, too. Caitrin also told Ollie if he wanted to run a tavern, he was going to have to get familiar with a stove. He burned the shit out of everything at first or put way too much salt, but he eventually figured it out.

Ollie was decent at cobbling together new recipes, but there was just this magic that happened when Caitrin and Lance did it. Lance grunted when I smacked him on the back.

"We'll be your taste testers, as usual."

"You're both hogs who like getting drunk."

"Yes, but we have exquisite taste."

"Did you get the stew started for the day?" Lance asked.

"Do you think this is my first day? Your momma trained me well."

"I have my doubts. You're still feral."

Ollie blushed and looked away. Lance was confusing. We *all* felt a pull to him. Ollie had it bad. Sometimes, it felt like Lance was flirting with us and other times, it felt like he wasn't into men at all. One day, I was going to crack the mystery that was Lance Argent, but I'd never do it in a way that busted up our friendship.

"I also set some bones and the vegetable parts I didn't need for the stew to boil so Caitrin could have some broth for her cough."

Lance's face softened. Fuck, he was just so pretty for a guy.

"Thanks. Can you two handle it for a while? I was going to get some honey and herbs from the market to see if it helps."

"Go. We have it covered," I said.

BECK

I had certain duties as the only child of the Madame. Yeah, I could have abandoned this place and left them to fend for themselves. Some of the men who frequented this place when I was a kid said being around all this was going to fuck me in the head, but you know what it did? I had a pretty healthy respect for women and hatred of men who abused them.

Some of the men who came from outside of Guttertown had the wrong idea. They came in here all swagger looking down on the women, but they were the ones who had to pay for sex. These were businesswomen profiting off of that, even the ones who had to come here because they were out of options. My mom took them in and took care of them.

I protected them when we were open, but I had errands when everyone was sleeping. There were the herbs to get, so no one ended up with a baby, restocking perfumes, creams, and ointments for the women. They gave my mom ten percent of what they earned to manage the house and pay their boarding and food. They kept the rest.

That ten percent also paid for what I was picking up today. It didn't sound like a lot, but the men of Guttertown kept their fucking mouths shut that they didn't pay the same rate as the rest of Nestran. The rest of Nestran wasn't going to admit they were frequenting Guttertown brothels, so *they* weren't discussing that my mom had tiers for them, too.

A merchant was going to pay more than a farmer, but the Barons were going to pay more than anyone. Guttertown women were onto them for the most part. They knew they'd stick around until their wife gave them an heir and then disappear. They'd make all kinds of promises they weren't going to keep.

Some still fell for it and thought it was going to be different with them. The Barons bought their sons here as a rite of passage and if none of the local women were falling for their shit, they'd pay for it and we'd be flush for months, sometimes the whole year.

I knew where I needed to go and was headed that way. I passed Neco Argent covered in blood and just gave him a nod. He nodded back. I didn't give a shit whose blood it was. Neco helped me look out for the girls. He might be a surly bastard who hated everyone, but he was actually a good guy.

And I was pretty sure he was a serial killer, but in a good way.

Neco and I couldn't be everywhere at once. Sometimes, the girls got hurt, and it got bad before we could get there and throw the man out. I'd banish them, but I'd hear talk their throats were slit.

I *could* have just thought they were shitty men who hurt women and someone outside of Nestran did the rest of us a favor, but a bag of gold and silver always mysteriously showed up in the girl's room the next morning.

It wasn't my mother, and it wasn't me. Neco had access,

and he was the only person I knew who moved like a panther and could sneak around the brothel without waking *me* up. I might hate how things went down between Lance and Neco, but he had my respect for protecting the girls.

On my way to the shop, I also ran into Lance. I wished I could make it right between those two, but I feared the damage had been done. Lance was distracted and walked straight into my chest. I grabbed him to steady him.

Lance unnerved me sometimes. He was shorter than the rest of us, but still a respectable height. The rest of us were pretty bulky. Ollie got big on the farm and I trained to fight with Neco so we could protect the girls. Ronan liked to swim to clear his head.

Lance was skinnier than us with lean muscles. You shouldn't underestimate him, though. He could throw a punch and kick someone out of his tavern with the best of us. He unnerved me because he was just so attractive and I couldn't do anything about it because he seemed only into women.

"Where's the fire?" I asked, steading him.

Lance didn't rush. He moved with a preternatural grace, like a predator. He was the smallest of us but also the most calculating. Lance knew he wouldn't win in brute strength, so be bided his time and looked for weaknesses. He'd kicked my arse more than once and he didn't even know how to use a sword. If he was in a hurry, something had spooked him and Lance didn't get scared much.

"Mom has a cough. It's getting worse. If the Pale Plague is back, then Guttertown healers can't do anything. I'd have to contact my father and I don't want to do that."

"Come on. We'll shop together."

All the Guttertown kids who hadn't been claimed by a Guttertown man refused to talk about their fathers, even if they knew who they were. It was like uttering their name would invoke them like a curse. They used and abused their kids.

I was probably the only kid in Guttertown who hadn't been claimed who *wasn't* a Baron's bastard. My mom never told me who he was because she never told him. My mom handpicked a man who had all the qualities she wanted, saw him exclusively, stopped taking her herbs, and then dumped him when she got pregnant.

Mom always said she wanted a kid, but she didn't want the man who sired it. I never got mad about it because my mom was a strong, multi-talented woman and I never felt like I was lacking in anything.

Still, my momma didn't raise an insensitive arsehole. I didn't just shop for the girls and use my body to protect them. Sometimes, they just needed to vent. I did that, too. They wouldn't talk to the other girls because some of them gossiped, but I'd keep my mouth shut. Neco let them vent to him sometimes, but he only responded in grunts back, so they usually came to me. I could do this with Lance.

The Pale Plague swept through Nestran about forty years ago and killed a ton of people. It hit Guttertown the hardest because we were the poorest. The Barons had access to the best healers. Their healers figured out how to cure it and then basically decided who lived and died.

Guttertown was quarantined and left to fend for itself until the plague died off. Our healers tried everything, but if they found the cure, they weren't totally sure about it. The Baron's healers were also pretty unethical for healers. To this day, a healer only learned the cure for the Pale Plague if they were going to be employed by a Baron.

The rest of Nestran didn't know it and the healers that did liked their money and privilege, so they didn't slip it to anyone else. Nestran hadn't seen the Pale Plague since before I was born, but any time someone started coughing, people talked because that was how it started.

"We haven't seen the Pale Plague in a long time. It could just be a cough. There has to be a least *one* talented healer in Nestran that would help you. They might do it for money. If all else fails, you could get them sloppy drunk with your experiment in the basement and one of the girls will seduce it out of him. They're all about the community and if it got Guttertown a cure for the Pale Plague, they'd do it in a heartbeat."

"Pussy and booze is going to be our best bet."

I laughed.

"That's the spirit. We could probably topple the Barony and have Guttertown running Nestran with that."

"That's because men are idiots when it comes to their cocks."

"Except you. That girl you were with the night we all lost our virginity keeps asking when you are coming back. You don't get stupid like the rest of us."

Seriously, Lance had exceptional control. Everyone else in our group got stupid over pretty girls *and* pretty men. Never Lance, even though both seemed to love him.

"Because I don't think of women like a wet hole, Beck."

"Neither do we."

"I know. Think there's any truth to the rumor that elderberry and honey tea helps with the Pale Plague?"

"Dunno, but it definitely helps with a cough. If it was the Pale Plague, you'd be coughing, too. It's pretty contagious. Caitrin could have just caught something because some arsehole came to drink when they were sick."

"I guess. You're one of the good ones, Beck." Lance sighed.

I tried not to preen because Lance was my friend and I didn't think he'd like it.

"One of the girls swears by peppermint and marshmallow root tea for a cough. I know where to buy the marshmallow root, but you've got peppermint growing in your courtyard. Ollie's dad planted it for the tavern."

"Yeah. I've been using it in my experiments."

"You going to have us over to taste it when it's ready?" Lance snorted.

"Yeah. You arseholes are my gauge for what the rest of Guttertown is going to like."

"The herbalist on the left has better prices than the herbalist on the right. They both have marshmallow root."

"The one on the right charges more because they aren't dicks."

I fell out laughing. That much was true, but you needed your wits about you in the Guttertown marketplace.

"The one on the right is nicer because they don't know shit and will probably poison you. Ilyn is gruff, but he knows his shit. The girls swear by him. And trust me, that's an endorsement you want."

It really was. They didn't just ask for herbs to prevent pregnancy or things to make them more beautiful. Sometimes, men brought disease into the house. Mom had a strict protocol for that. It had to be reported so we could trace it back to which man brought it in to ban him, then the girl couldn't work until she was treated.

And the Barons might have cornered the market on treating the Pale Plague and wouldn't tell anyone, but it was Guttertown who figured out how to treat it if you caught something in the bedroom. Ilyn *could* have been a healer. His father was, and he trained him, his brother, and his sister. Ilyn had a queasy stomach, so his brother and sister were healers and Ilyn became an herbalist. Ilyn's brother and sister sent their patients to him to buy what they needed, but if you weren't going to stick a festering wound in his face, Ilyn could help, too.

"So does Mom, but I went in there to get something for the pain after Neco broke my nose. He yelled at me and kicked me out."

Ugh. If I could fix that, I would. Lance's nose had been

reset, but the relationship between Lance and Neco was shattered.

"You didn't walk in there with blood on your face, did you?"

"Well, yeah. It fucking hurt. I was more worried about the pain than the blood."

"That'll do it. Ilyn doesn't like blood or gore, but he loves a challenge. You're presentable right now. Ask him about the cough. You'll have a much different conversation."

"Thanks, Beck," Lance said, giving me a side hug.

We were all secure men who were big on hugging except for Lance. If you tried to give Lance a proper hug, he'd side step you for a side hug. Which was weird because he hugged Caitrin properly all the time.

"I have to hit Ilyn up for my order. I'll tag along."

"You're the best."

I always wanted to puff up and preen when Lance complimented me and it was going to lead to me blowing up this friendship and getting my heart broken.

LUCY

Pretending to be a boy was a lot more complicated at twenty than it was before I knew I was a girl. It all started when they got hot and we all got interested in the opposite sex. There was that time Ollie wanted to lose his virginity and roped everyone into saving some coins so we could do that at the brothel.

It wasn't just embarrassing because I didn't have a dick. The Madame was like our second mother and most of those girls looked out for us. Apparently, I was the only one who felt weird about that.

I wasn't completely dead from the waist down. When I was alone at night, I explored my body and figured out what I liked. I kind of had to because I got urges being around my friends and it wasn't like I could ever act on them without blowing up my secret.

So, when I had Asha alone, I didn't let her touch me or get me naked. I touched her how I wanted to be touched and then I rubbed her back while we just chatted. I figured she needed a break from pleasuring men and I actually learned a lot on the subject considering I'd probably never do it.

It didn't help that my best friends were good men, and I was in love with all of them. They were supportive and amazing to talk to. I just reacted badly when Ollie flirted with me.

Like, take Beck. He could take *any* situation and make you feel like it wasn't going to be the end of the world. He usually had a solution, so it wasn't, either. Beck was also very easy to look at.

Most humans migrated to Nestran from Idric Island, where the weather was so shitty, you could only grow certain things, but some of us came from the smaller islands surrounding Idric. Beck's ancestors came from one of the smaller islands and settled in Guttertown. Guttertown was really a mesh of culture because we had a lot of people from the smaller islands that the rest of Nestran didn't want.

Beck and the Madame had dark skin and hadn't cut their hair since they were born. They twisted it into locs and wore beads in their hair. The Madame had a sword made for him that wasn't a broad sword like the rest of Nestran used. This one was curved and the training to use it had been passed down through men from their island.

I couldn't watch Beck with his shirt off when he was training. My mouth got dry and my pussy got wet, but that wasn't the problem. My nipples also got hard. My breasts were firmly smashed down with bandages and I still felt like it was glaringly obvious.

It was still hard to walk away. It was easier when Neco fucking Argent was training with him. We'd sneak into each other's rooms and talk all night.

Neco had been dealing with shit when his father came back and I was there for him. I was probably closer to Neco than all of them. He had been gutted when his mom got pregnant with his sister and they had to go live in the brothel.

While *all* of that was going on, my body was in the process of trying to have its first period and I was a little emotional.

When we heard Neco had been attacked protecting his mom, we all went to him. He shut us out and told us he couldn't be friends with us anymore because he had to focus on protecting his mom and sister.

I tried to sneak into his new room that night to talk to him and the window was bolted shut. Even if it was closed, it was never locked so I could get in. I tried tapping on the window, but he ignored me.

I went home and cried myself to sleep. A regular person would have given Neco space and let him know we'd always be there for him. We'd help him protect his mom and sister, too, because we were his friends.

But I wasn't a regular person at that time. I was a ten-year-old who thought they were boy and had no idea why *everything* was upsetting me more than usual.

At school the next day, some of the kids were saying nasty things to him because of his eye. I said something and instantly regretted it. Neco looked at me like I'd slapped him and I knew I was wrong. That wasn't me.

I chased after Neco trying to apologize and as soon as I got close, he whirled around, broke my nose, and told me to stay away from him. Neco and me had been enemies ever since. I knew I was wrong and Neco was going through some stuff, but Neco was wrong, too. He never came back to us; like we meant nothing to him.

He trained with Beck to protect the girls and half-assed spoke to Ollie at the tavern because we had the best drink in Guttertown, but he just pretended Ronan didn't exist and he was straight up hostile to me.

Just seeing him today pissed me off.

But I focused on Beck. Beck was massive and looked dangerous, but he also had this soothing nature. There were still parts of me that *felt* like a boy but I realized a lot of me had been girl all along. Like, I'd probably never be ladylike and refined, but I really wanted to stroll through the streets of Guttertown holding Beck's hand like I was his girlfriend.

Still, I couldn't.

I hadn't been in this shop since this man yelled at me. I'd overreacted about plenty of shit, but I was perfectly within my right to storm out of this shop and never come back when this man yelled at a ten-year-old with a broken nose. Fuck the fact that my body was trying to have its first period. That was just mean.

Ilyn was older when I walked in, but from the way he was looking at me, I felt like that ten-year-old with a broken nose again.

"Beck. Glad to see your friend has grown out of getting his nose broken."

"Fuck you," I snarled.

Beck caught the back of my shirt and hauled me back. Yeah, that was one of the things left over from thinking I was a boy. Now that I was older, I was usually calculating and watched people before I made any moves. But sometimes, I just snapped and really wanted to punch someone in the face. This man made an awful day even worse. My period started the night I got home.

Ilyn was associated with one of the worst days of my life and the irrational part of my brain just really wanted to punch him in the face since I couldn't deck Neco. Neco got massive, scary, and annoyingly sexy. He also broke my nose and thought I was a man. I wasn't starting a fistfight with him.

"Sorry, my good friend was having a bad day when he showed up covered in blood and doesn't like to be reminded of it."

"I'd been having a good day until he got blood on my floor."

"Ilyn, you're just being a miserable cunt at this point. His mom is sick."

The old man's eyes brightened, and he finally looked like he was ready to stop giving me a hard time.

"Tell me."

"She has a cough and sometimes, it's like she can't take her breath. I know the Pale Plague started with a cough."

"It's not the plague. My brother would have told me and I'd be seeing more people asking about it. You're the second person asking about a cough, so that's not an epidemic. The plague was highly contagious, so you'd be coughing, too."

I let out my breath.

"Do you have anything it could be?"

"Could be the lungs or the stomach. You wouldn't think it's the stomach, but the stomach has acid and sometimes, it acts up. It'll cause a cough at night or after meals."

"I haven't noticed that. It seems like all the time, but I also didn't know I needed to look for that."

"Chamomile is going to help either way as is ginger. You could do a double whammy for her stomach and her lungs if you do a spicy, ginger-garlic soup. Can you cook, boy?"

"Caitrin's boy knows damned well how to cook," Beck said, smacking me on the back. "He's responsible for a good bit of the new recipes coming out of the Whispering Raven, booze and food."

"No shit? The boy who bled on my floor? I've got the chamomile, but fresh ginger is best. I've got it dried and ground, but for the soup, you're going to want to dig it out of the ground. There's plenty around here because we have all these infernal mangoes.

"Also, Theda's boy was in here earlier because his mother also has a cough. There might be others with minor coughs that are seeking herbalists instead of a healer because it's not serious just yet. Instead of coming to me, they are going to that snake oil salesman across the street who will poison them with a smile while promising to make their cock harder for longer. The Whispering Raven is known for their food and their spirits. If you're putting soup to the pot for your mother, put a big one on for everyone just in case."

I might hate Neco, but Theda had always been amazing to us as kids. Neco hated me right back, but his mom was one of the few people he'd die for.

He wouldn't dump a soup that could help his mom just because I made it, right?

NECO

I felt slightly better. Momma wouldn't go to a healer, even with the bag of coins I found, because she didn't think it was serious. Maybe it wasn't, but she and Rowena were all I had in this world and I couldn't kill anything to protect her from a cough. I was allowed to overreact just in case.

I went straight to Ilyn. Every intelligent person knew he was the best. So did Ilyn, that's why he was a miserable arsehole to everyone. As a fellow miserable arsehole, he was a kindred spirit.

I didn't much give a shit about going into Ollie's tavern with animal blood on my shirt, but I definitely took it off to talk to Ilyn. Ilyn didn't give a shit my chest was bare but he would have been pissed if I came into his shop with blood on me. I could respect that.

If you wanted real herbal knowledge that was going to do what it was supposed to, you went to Ilyn. If you wanted smoke blown up your arse with a big smile and to end up pissing blood, you went to Derwin. Some people *kept* going back to Derwin after all that because they swore their dick was harder for five seconds longer than usual.

Some men were fucking stupid.

Still, I knew for sure it wasn't the Pale Plague and what to watch for. I also knew what things to get her to eat and drink. The *only* reason I had her baking Rowena's cake with her cough was because while I was a decent cook, but I was shit at baking. The last time I tried to bake a cake for Rowena or Momma, it was ugly as fuck, caved in the middle, and tasted terrible.

Ollie's aunt and uncle were decent people or I wouldn't have let Rowena around them. They'd been great to me when I was a kid. I lost a lot of people when I decided I needed to be able to protect my family and anyone working at the brothel.

After we left school, everyone went to learn a trade, but I took a very special kind of apprenticeship. The island Beck and the Madame's ancestors came from had all kinds of skills they brought with them. They passed them down to their descendants, even if they didn't teach the rest of Guttertown. The Madame's brother was the brothel bodyguard before Beck and he trained Beck in the scimitar he carried.

I asked him for something else. The man that beat me and took my eye got banished, but that was about all Guttertown could do. Panas couldn't even really hit him when he was pulling him off of me and throwing him out. If he made a stink, it would have been Panas that got thrown in jail.

Panas was a warrior. If it were a Guttertown man cutting up, he beat the shit out of them. It couldn't sit right with him that the other men could lay hands on our women and not pay. I wanted him to help me make them pay and not get caught.

Panas couldn't help me, but their sister could. She was a trained assassin. Okay, mostly she ran a bakery, but she'd been taught the art. Keeva taught me. I *had* to cut everyone from my life to learn those skills. I needed to focus because being bad at killing people was how I got caught. And if I got caught, they'd punish Momma and Rowena.

I may have eventually found my way back to them once I knew what I was doing, but fucking Lance decided to implode our relationship by joining the boys taunting me. I had been closer to him than any of them and told him things I didn't tell anyone else. Clearly, that meant nothing to him and they all sided with Lance.

Fuck them.

I wanted to focus on Rowena today and not my past. I had the boar roasting while making small talk with Ollie's uncle. His aunt was in the kitchen helping bake the cake. My sister was off somewhere with Baryn, but I wasn't worried about her. She could handle herself against kids her own age.

"Listen, I wanted to talk to you about your sister," Tade said. "I know it's not considered proper in the rest of Nestran, but we do things differently here. She has a gift with animals. It's rare and Rowena is a natural. She has this calming effect on them.

"Some of the merchants from the Trulos District like to pretend they aren't getting their horses in Guttertown, but mine are on par with the Barons'. It takes a special kind of person to break a horse so it can be trained and sold. Baryn isn't suited. He already knows this. He's better suited to crops and the other livestock. Baryn is crazy for Rowena and so are the rest of us. I'd love to apprentice her for the horses."

Rowena would love that, but I also knew my sister often didn't know what the fuck she wanted. Her favorite color seemed to change every other day. She'd request the same meal several times a week and then decide she didn't want it anymore.

I loved my sister but ten-year-old girls were confusing as fuck.

"I think it's a great idea, but it's up to her."

"She already said she wanted to, but it was up to you."

I grinned. Tade was right for asking her before he asked me. I'd never force her into anything. Rowena telling him it was up to me was Rowena speak for her being a little terror if I said no. I mean, I was the one who taught her to use her fists, but the girls at the brothel taught her to use her wits against men, too.

And I knew my sister. If I said no, she'd have every girl in the brothel on my arse *and* she'd punch me in the dick.

"Then, I guess you have a new horse trainer. You don't tell Rowena Argent what to do."

Tade grinned.

"Oh, we're all quite aware. How do you think we found out she's good with the stallions?"

I sighed.

"She didn't hit you, did she?"

Because this was a great opportunity for her. I told her not to start anything, but to finish it. I was pretty sure she did that outside the house, but she had no problem punching me. And if she thought someone hurt me, she'd punch them, too.

I saw Ollie coming and had no idea why he had Ronan with him. Beck and Ollie said I had every right to hit Lance for what he said to me, but wanted me to make peace. Ronan was different. Ronan thought I should have let it go, heard him out, and forgiven him. Ronan actually thought I *shouldn't* have hit Lance. It was a betrayal, so I pretended like Ronan didn't exist.

The Whispering Raven had amazing herbed crusty bread. It sucked when I wanted some and fucking Lance was working the front of the house because I had to leave. Things tended to devolve into shouting matches and I really didn't want to get banned from the Whispering Raven because I hit him again.

Ollie had a sack full of bread with him for the party. I appreciated the bread. Momma and Rowena loved it, but I would have preferred he leave Ronan where he found him. Ronan had something large and flat on his back. I didn't particularly give a shit what was in it.

"Ollie, can I talk to you?" I yelled.

It was implied I wanted to talk to him alone, but I also thought Ollie knew better than to bring Ronan to my sister's birthday. Was Lance busy? Just bring all my enemies, why didn't he.

"Okay, hear me out," Ollie said.

Ugh. I *should* be punching him in the face, but then his uncle might kick us off his land. And frankly, Ollie's face was too beautiful to maim.

"You have five seconds."

"Ronan is an artist. He just got shafted by a Baron and was at the Whispering Raven after you to pick up some shifts since he lost that commission. Guttertown kids don't get art. We get stories told to us by our families, but we don't get the illustrated books like the rest of Nestran.

"I thought it would be really neat to have someone at Rowena's party who could draw pictures of them however they wanted. Like, if they just wanted a portrait or maybe draw them as a character in their favorite story. I thought Rowena would like one standing on the bones of her enemies. Ronan thought it was a great idea and agreed to do it for free."

Ugh. I didn't particularly want to forgive Ronan. I didn't forgive and forget. I held grudges. But that was actually amazing. Rowena would love it and so would the other kids her age. Guttertown didn't get portraits done like the rest of Nestran. They only existed if a family member had the talent and time to make one. Plenty of Guttertown had talent, but with trying to stay fed, housed, and the paying fucking taxes the Barons rained down on us, time was something a lot of people didn't have.

Ronan wouldn't have a lot of time, either, but he agreed to do this. He'd lost a ton of money from a Baron and he wasn't asking for payment. And I hadn't looked at him or said a single word to him in the last ten years. Ronan was a good guy.

Maybe this particular grudge needed to go. I was older now. I could see that Ronan had been in an impossible situation. All of us had been thick as thieves until I lost my eye. I knew they wanted me back, but Lance hurt me and I hurt Lance back. No matter how they handled it, they would have lost one of us.

I pushed them all away, but I punished Ronan for picking Lance. I could admit when I was wrong.

Lance Argent was still my enemy, though.

LUCY

I might hate Neco, but I wasn't going to ruin his sister's name day. We could spare Ronan. I sent Ollie with several loaves of bread and he was supposed to come back and help since we told Mom she had to rest. If we told her it was Rowena's name day, she would have come down and tried to run the tavern.

It would be mostly slow until everyone got off of work, but we'd still have people come in. Ollie's broth was ready, so I moved it off the fire and started a garlic ginger soup to cook. Ilyn was right. There could be more people, so I made a lot of it.

I cut a piece of crusty bread, smeared it with butter, and made a bowl of broth to bring up to Mom. She was upstairs darning our socks. She saw the look I was giving her.

"I've got a cough. I'm not dead."

"Don't say that," I said, making the gesture to ward off evil.

"You've always been way too serious, my one and only."

"Ollie made broth, and I made bread. He bought butter from their farm."

"Ugh. His aunt makes the best butter. Did you at least thank Ollie?"

Mom really wanted Ollie and me together, but I'd seen it go down before. The Barons didn't care if their daughters were with someone. If they ever needed anything from them, they expected them to pay them back at the brothels. Not all men were okay with that. And the Barons never actually gave their daughters a sum they needed to work off. It was just never paid until they couldn't work anymore.

If I could get us secure with my experiments in the basement, I wouldn't have to worry about asking my father for money and *maybe* I could tell my friends. There was always the possibility of a fucking disaster that was well beyond our means, though.

"I'm not a savage. Of course, I did."

She just laughed.

"You are when it comes to your friends."

Yeah, Mom saw right through me and knew it wasn't just Ollie. I was just around him the most.

"You're terrible," I laughed.

"No, I know you. I panicked when you came out a girl because I know what happens to daughters of Barons. I thought I was doing right raising you as a boy until I couldn't anymore. Maybe that was a mistake, but I don't regret the friends you made. I took your choice away once and I won't do it again. They are safe men to tell."

"I know. But if I ever have to ask him for help and he finds out I'm a girl, it's going to be the brothel. They'll do something stupid and get themselves killed."

Mom just looked at me sadly. She was about to say something when there was a crash downstairs. I told her to stay and eat while I went flying to check it out. Most people didn't get drunk and break things until much later.

Autar was sitting at a table with his face in his hands and had thrown his tankard against the wall. It was metal, so it didn't break. Ollie looked like he was five seconds from tossing Autar out, but Autar was a good guy. He was *massive*. Probably bigger than Neco, but he was a huge flirt and was always asking women to marry him. He was usually harmless. Part of running a tavern was figuring out when to toss people and went to listen. I had a feeling Autar needed an ear.

I plopped next to him.

"What's wrong and why are you throwing my tankards?"

The big guy looked up at me with red eyes. I wasn't going to say a damned thing about a man crying. If anything, more of them should.

"It's my father."

Autar grew up on one of the farms. He'd always been big, but working the land and with the animals had bulked him up. He was also a gentle giant who was good with animals.

"Is he sick?"

I immediately thought to my mom's cough.

"No, they *lied* to me. My mom and dad were married and running the farm when fucking Folcard showed up for something. My dad stepped out to get it and Folcard raped my mom. *They* aren't sure if I'm my dad or Folcard's, but Folcard came back and decided I was his. He claims I look exactly like the paintings of his ancestors, which he refuses to show as proof. He wants to use my size to turn me into his general. If I refuse, he's going to tax our farm out of existence."

Fucking Folcard. With everything I knew about him, that didn't shock me. And I couldn't throw my arms around Autar and hug him. If Folcard was his father, then that meant Autar was my half-brother.

I didn't particularly care to ever have any contact with my father. I don't think any of the Argent kids did, but we were all curious about our siblings. Most of us were only children. Neco was pretty unique with Rowena.

Still, it was this unspoken rule. Even if you knew, you didn't speak their name. It was like even speaking it was like cursing yourself. So, we'd wonder if we were related and compare features, but we never said the name out loud unless we had to.

Autar was being vulnerable right now. He could have told me anything. Folcard taxing his parents and forcing him into the service would have sufficed without telling me Folcard violated his mother and was possibly his father.

"Can I tell you a secret that might make that utter shite fucker possibly being your father slightly better? At least, I hope it will."

"What would make me feel best would be feeding him to our pigs, but I'm willing to try anything at this point."

"You have to make an oath with me not to tell anyone."

"I swear."

"Folcard is *definitely* my father. We might be half-siblings."

"No shit? How'd you end up so scrawny then?"

"Shut the fuck up. I'm magnificent."

"Magnificently puny."

"While you were shoveling shit, I was tossing drunks out of this tavern when we got out of school. You want to throw down with someone who could manage a raging drunk at thirteen?"

Autar snorted.

"Fuck, no. And if Folcard had any sense, he wouldn't want me as his general. I might be big, but I *hate* conflict. This is terrible. And I'm going to have to be around him *knowing* what he did to my mom and I can't do a damned thing about it."

"You can come back here for a drink and some food while we talk shit about him. It's not as satisfying as breaking his nose, but I'm *really* good at insulting people who deserve it."

"And the food is good, the spirits get you drunk, and all the pretty women drink here."

I rolled my eyes.

"One of them is going to dump their drink on you and hit you one of these days."

Autar winked at me.

"Who's to say they haven't when you weren't working? Eventually, one of them will marry me."

"You have to earn it and be serious when you ask first."

"I am. Sometimes, I see a pretty, sassy woman and I want her to be my wife. She says no and then ten minutes later, I see another pretty sassy woman who is also wife material, so I ask."

"No one wants to be proposed to by a giant drunk man in a tavern. It either needs to be special or a mutually beneficial arrangement."

Autar's eyes narrowed at me.

"Pretty sure you don't understand women any better than I do. *No one* knows what they want."

I rolled my eyes.

"They are all just as varied as men and you can find out what they want by doing what you do with other men. You *ask* them."

"I'm pretty sure you're wrong about that."

Ugh. You got to see both sides of things when you were a woman pretending to be a man. I certainly got treated differently because no one thought I was a woman. We weren't all that different, there were just certain things expected of us and some physical limitations.

I could hunt just as well as Autar could, but I didn't own a horse to get large kills home and our donkey was too stubborn to take hunting. Once he learned how, Ollie was a fantastic cook. Beck was just as much a den mother to the girls as the Madame was.

And I couldn't explain any of that to my possible half-brother because he wouldn't believe me unless I told him *how* I knew all that.

"Just trust me. Talk to them like you talk to your guy friends."

"No way. My guy friends are super ugly and they don't smell good like women. I'd be lying if I told them they were pretty and I liked their smell. They'd probably kick my arse, too. You're kinda pretty for a guy and you don't stink, but you might be my brother and that's weird. You should also consider it a compliment that I said you're not ugly like most men because we're all hideous."

"You're just only attracted to women, and that's okay."

"I can't tell my guy friends they have superb tits. They'll hit me."

I snorted.

"You say that to the wrong woman and she'll hit you, too."

"Man, you don't understand women *at all*, Lance. Every woman loves it when you compliment her tits."

He didn't get it, so *I* hit him on behalf of all women. He'd think it was just a little brother thing, but I hope he at least got the message.

"Okay, okay! Don't beat me. I'll take it under advisement next time I see a woman with glorious tits."

"Seriously, when you're not working for Folcard, come in to eat and drink. We should get to know each other better now that we know we might be related and I want to watch when a woman with magnificent tits kicks your arse in my tavern."

"How about we place a wager? If that big-tittied woman ever kicks my arse in your bar, I'll set up something between your tavern and our farm."

"And if you win?"

My half-brother just grinned at me.

"I talk a *lot* but I'm rarely serious. I know you're right, but I'm going to make you earn it."

I fell out laughing. Autar was a few years older than me, so

I wasn't as close to him as I was with my friends. He drank a lot in our tavern and he got along with everyone, me included.

"I hate that your whole life imploded, but it's kind of cool you might be my brother. My mom always liked you."

"Oh, your mom has *beautiful* tits."

I knew he was just giving me a hard time, so I hit him again. I would have hit him for that even if he knew I was really his half-sister.

OLIVER

I always felt like a big man when one of my plots worked and none of us spent a night in the cells. Caitrin would have my arse if I landed Lance in the cells again. She'd probably box my ears if *I* ended up there, too.

But I didn't have to tumble with the law this time. I just had to take the risk that Neco wouldn't implode his little sister's name day by gutting Ronan for showing up and me for bringing him. I just figured Neco loved his sister, and he hadn't left any evidence yet, so there was a good chance he wouldn't kill us in front of witnesses.

I suppose he could always kill us in our sleep, but it ended up working out in the end. Ronan and Neco were at least being civil when I left. I was waiting for Ronan to come back from the party when Autar came in. He was a good guy, but he threw a tankard at my head, so I was about to toss him.

Lance swooped in and I could have sworn Lance was flirting with him. Lance was laughing and hitting him. I hadn't seen Lance look that happy in a long time. I was a little irritated about it because Lance never smiled at me like that. It was just that Autar was very much into women. I was pretty sure Autar fell in love with every semi-attractive woman who said hello to him

Before I could even think about it, our rush started spilling in because everyone was getting off of work. I went behind the bar and Lance started taking orders. A few of the regulars took a seat where I could keep the drinks coming.

I saw an outsider come in. He wasn't dressed like a Baron but he wasn't poorly dressed like he didn't have money. Probably a merchant looking for the brothel. He sat at the bar and looked utterly lost.

"Can I help you, friend?"

He slid four gold coins across the bar. That was way more than anything in here cost.

"Ale and information."

Sure, buddy. I didn't share Guttertown secrets to outsiders for gold. I'd take in what he wanted and probably lie about it. I got his ale and slid it over. He took a sip like he was expecting piss, but then his eyes lit up.

"This isn't half bad."

Dick. Caitrin and Lance made the best ale in Nestran. He could at least say that. I cocked an eyebrow at him.

"Has the Blight hit Guttertown yet?" he asked, leaning in conspiratorially.

Fuck me. Guttertown couldn't handle a blight. Even if our crops weren't hit, the Barons and merchants would swoop in and take our food. We'd starve anyway.

"Tell me what you know and I'll tell you what I know," I said.

My momma and aunt didn't raise no fool.

"They're calling him The Blight. He comes out of nowhere and slits your throat. No one knows who he is or why he's doing it. The Blight never leaves any clues behind and he doesn't take anything. It doesn't make sense!"

Ah. They'd given Neco a handy, little serial-killer name. At least, I was pretty sure it was Neco because I'd talked to Beck and we'd compared notes. We'd never actually *seen* Neco standing over a body. I didn't think we ever would. And if we did, it would probably be the last thing we ever saw.

Neco might have pulled away from us, but he was still a friend. And he was doing good work. Most of the men who visited brothels gave fake names except for the Barons, but they'd mention their trade to the girls. We might not be able to match up the names, but if someone mentioned a trade, I could confirm it with Beck.

I needed to protect Neco.

"Oh, yeah. We didn't have a name for him, but he started here. We don't think he lives here. Our houses are too close together and we know everyone. He picked off some people that were a little easier to get to. Probably to practice his trade on people the rest of Nestran wouldn't miss and then moved on. He's not one of us. We're up in everyone's business here and know when someone isn't right. We never could figure out why he was doing it, either. He didn't want anything, and the victims were all different. He left as quickly as he came. No one has been murdered like that in a while."

Neco better kiss my arse for this because I was going to have to figure out how to get the rest of Guttertown on this ruse so they didn't think it was me. It was one thing to end up in the cells for some harmless fun. They'd execute me if they thought I was butchering merchants and I *wasn't* prepared for that like Neco was.

The man nodded and drained his ale.

"I'm not a guard. I'm who they call to figure out where to point them. You ever see anyone in here late at night covered in blood?"

"Not like that, but if someone is killing outside of Guttertown, the chances of them making it through the Trulos District and the markets to get back here with blood on them without getting caught is going to be pretty slim. You have to walk near the palace to get from the Trulos District to Guttertown and the rest of Nestran has a lot more guards than we do. He'd need to pass through Lower Cutwart. They don't have a brothel, so they come here, but they do have two taverns. Drunk people are out late. Someone would see him."

"What's your name, kid?"

"Oliver. My friends call me Ollie."

"Well, Oliver, I'm Inspector Trevils. You've got some keen insights for a tavern keeper. You'd make a hell of a deputy. You're being wasted here slinging ale, but I know how this world works. If you see anything, find me," he said, getting up to leave.

What was the world coming to when I actually kind of liked a Nestran inspector? He didn't assume I wanted him to call me Ollie and instead of coming here and cracking my head for this information, he paid me pretty fucking well for it. He stroked my ego a bit and didn't act like he was better than me because I lived in Guttertown.

I almost felt bad lying straight to his face, but if I told him those men died because they abused Guttertown women at the brothel, nothing would happen. Even if he *wanted* to do something about it, he reported his findings to the Barons and *they* decided if the guards busted heads.

Still, I knew how to handle it. Guttertown protected our own. If the people knew someone was fighting back when Nestran hurt us, they wouldn't need a name. I wasn't lying about everyone being up in everyone's business. I knew some shit I didn't particularly want to know. But a vigilante getting justice? We were hardly educated, but we weren't stupid. People would happily look the other way and not dig into it.

A brothel and a tavern could *easily* handle this.

LUCY

The tavern had been packed until we closed, but it generally was. It kept us clothed and fed, so I wasn't complaining about it at all, even if running around bringing food and drinks to people while running back to the kitchen to check on the garlic and ginger soup I had going had my feet and back killing me by the end of the night.

My night wasn't done yet. I made enough soup to feed the tavern the next day, but some of it was already earmarked for two people. I set aside some for my mom and steeled myself to bring some to the brothel for Theda.

I would have asked Ollie or Beck, but Beck hadn't come by and Ollie was up to some kind of Ollie shenanigans and Mom got mad last time we spent the night in the cells. Neco acted like Ronan didn't exist, so if I sent him with soup, it wasn't going to get to Theda.

Neco and I were different. We avoided each other, but when we couldn't, it ended up in a screaming match. He left the tavern if I was working the front of the house and I avoided him if I was at the brothel for Beck.

Thing was, I could *destroy* Neco Argent by telling him my

secret. He imploded our friendship to step up for his mom and her new baby. He grew into a man who took hurting women and kids seriously. That was the one thing I liked about him. If he knew he broke a girl's nose he wouldn't be able to deal with it.

It wasn't worth the hassle of anyone finding out my secret.

So, I just walked over to the brothel with the soup and braced myself. If that fucker hit me again, he was going to need one of the Baron's healers to extract his testicles from his stomach. I was serious. I had been so shocked he hit me when we were ten that I just stood there when he stomped off.

I had ten years of rage built up against Neco Argent and he really deserved a broken nose from me. But first? Soup.

The brothel stayed open much later than the tavern. We *could* have brought in more coin feeding the merchants slinking off in the dead of night, but we were doing well without it. Some of those men were insufferable, and I got my love of sleeping from my mom.

Neco saw me. He scowled at me but I knew he thought I was here for Beck. I generally was. He stood up clenching his fists when he realized I was headed straight for him. Yeah, he looked ready to hit me again.

"Listen, first of all, fuck you. Secondly, I have hot soup in my hands that I have no problem throwing in your face but I made it for Theda because Ilyn said she had a cough like my mom."

"Fuck you back. Ilyn should learn to keep his mouth shut."

"Listen, shit for brains. I can't stand you, but I adore Theda and Rowena is a good kid. I don't particularly care if we both die hating each other, but your mom and sister didn't shut me out and break my nose.

"Ilyn said the cough could be one of two things and this soup would help both. If it's more serious, they'll need a healer. You know what's going to happen if you have to ask your father. He might be satisfied with you, but he might want payment from Rowena, too, and no one can stop him.

"If you go after him, you'll end up dead either way and they'll take it out on Theda and Rowena. The Madame can't say no or they'll shut her down. All the girls would be homeless and unable to work until she agreed to his demands.

"So, take the soup, you knob head. There's enough for you and Rowena just in case its contagious. I only made enough for you so you don't give it back to them if it goes away."

Neco snatched the soup away from me and glared down at me.

"This doesn't make things right between us," he snapped.

Fuck him. If he wasn't holding soup I needed to get to Theda and Rowena and my mom would need that pot back, I'd return the favor and break his fucking nose.

"First of all, this wasn't a peace offering, you utter shit. Your mom was like a second mother to me once. I already apologized for what I said to you. As far as I'm concerned, *you* owe *me* an apology for cutting me out and then breaking my nose."

"What the fuck would I apologize to you for? I had every right to hit you. In fact, I'd like to hit you again," he said, setting the soup down.

I cracked my neck and bounced on the balls of my feet. I was probably about to get my arse kicked, but I'd get at least one good punch in. I'd feel like shit tomorrow, but if I could just break his nose, I'd feel much better.

But Rowena zipped between us and thumped me right in the boob. Fuck! Getting punched in the tit hurt, even if they were strapped down. My eyes watered and I tried not to let them know *why* it hurt me.

Neco grabbed Rowena and pulled her behind him.

"Don't you *dare* think about hurting my sister!" he roared.

Beck came barreling in next and yanked me away.

"Shit, Lance. You know Neco gets feral about his sister. What were you doing?"

"I wasn't trying to hurt Rowena. I brought Theda some soup and Neco started shit."

Beck pulled me to his bedroom.

"Neco would have finished it, too. Don't mess with him. I mean it."

"Maybe *he* shouldn't fuck with *me.*"

"Look, you did good bringing Theda soup. I know you were just trying to help, but maybe you should have had me do it."

"You weren't at the tavern."

I suppose I could have found Beck instead of Neco, but Beck was needed to protect the girls and Neco was right there.

"I *hate* him."

"No, you don't."

"I really do."

I'd loved Neco once, but he hurt me, so I hurt him back. When I felt like shit about that and tried to apologize, he hurt me *again.* No, I really hated him. And I hated that I hated him because we'd been so close before. I got a lot of joy out of hating my father and shit-talking him, but it hurt to hate Neco. Which just pissed me off.

"Look, Ollie tricked him into making peace with Ronan at the party. You and Neco are the last holdouts from our group."

Ugh. Neco and Ronan made peace? I'd never ask them to choose between us, but now I was the outsider. Then again, Neco didn't want to make peace with me. Beck saw me glaring at him.

"Look, none of us are going to force either of you to do anything. But we were a group once and there's been a piece missing since Neco left."

I ran my hands through my short hair. I was trying not to get irritated with Beck because I really did love him.

"Why are you talking to me and not Neco? He's the one who pulled away."

"I'm planning on that after you leave."

"Well, I'm leaving now. I did what I came here to do and my mom is sick, too."

"Take care of Caitrin, Lance."

Yeah, Mom was my life. I'd always take care of her. Ten-year-old me missed Neco, but I was twenty now. I'd grown up.

Neco Argent could get fucked.

NECO

Lance Argent needed to stay the fuck away from me. I appreciated the soup for Momma, but he could have sent it through Beck or Ollie. Even Ronan would have been better. I'd forgiven Ronan.

He'd drawn for hours and didn't take a break until the kids stopped asking for drawings. If someone wanted more than one, Ronan happily did it. He must have done at least five for Rowena alone that were now hanging in her bedroom and she couldn't stop talking about them. Ronan had grown into a good man as far as I was concerned.

And then there was Lance. I don't think *any* of them understood why I was so mad at him. Lance and I were both Argents. I knew who my father was because he came back around, but Lance wouldn't unless Caitrin told him.

We *could* have been half-brothers, and we bonded over that. We snuck into each other's rooms at night and would stay up talking. And that was when it happened. Lance Argent became my first crush.

I pushed everyone away because I needed to focus on learning to protect my family if we were going to be living in the brothel. I locked my window to keep Lance out and ignored him when he knocked because I was an idiot ten-year-old who wanted to have their first kiss with someone who might be their half-brother.

And then when I came back to school, some kids were making fun of me because I got my arse beat and lost an eye. I hadn't learned to fight back, and I hadn't hit my growth spurt yet. I was still pretty small and scrawny. I'd been planning to walk away and bide my time, but then Lance joined in.

It hurt like fuck. Outside of my family, I'd been the closest to Lance. I thought punching Lance in the face would make me feel better and kill that crush, but it didn't. I went home and it still hurt.

I left my window open that night to see if he'd come back. We could talk it out and move on. I could explain to him why I needed space to train for now, but I might eventually be able to make my way back to all of them. Lance never came.

And Lance kept getting more beautiful every year. It was unfair for a man to look like that. He wasn't too masculine, and he had a little bit of a feminine look about him. It could confuse people, but if they tried to do anything to Lance, he was a pretty good fighter.

Seeing Lance set me into this rage. Moreso than the rest of my friends because they didn't hurt me like he did and that stupid childhood crush never went away. I still wanted to know what it felt like to kiss Lance and that very much couldn't happen until I knew we weren't related.

So, I'd been trying really hard to convince myself that Lance was a terrible person who hit at me during one of my worst moments and he wasn't worth my feelings. Then, he did shit like bring us soup because Momma was sick.

Ugh. I'd feel a lot better if I could kill someone, but Keeva drilled it into me that an assassin without a code was just a serial killer. Serial killers usually made mistakes and got caught.

I couldn't kill someone because I was having a bad day. If I let emotion get involved, I'd fuck something up.

My family was eating the soup, and I slipped out of our rooms. I didn't know where I was going or what I was going to do, but Lance lived next door in the tavern and that just seemed too close right now.

I went to storm out, but Beck found me and pounced. Since we lived in the same building, I was closer to Beck than I was with my old friends now. We protected the girls together and Beck took care of all of them, my mom and Rowena included.

"You look like you're ready to do something stupid and end up in the cells. Come spar with me."

We were both trained by his uncle in fighting, but I took additional lessons with Keeva that he didn't really know about. I was almost certain Beck didn't know his aunt who baked the best sweets in Guttertown could slit a man's throat without anyone in his house knowing.

Yeah, that would do. We were pretty evenly matched with our fists. I was bigger than Beck, but Beck was faster than me. We walked to the courtyard and took our shirts off. Lance was beautiful in this ethereal androgynous way, but Beck was pretty in a dangerous way.

His skin was dark and his body roped with muscle. His hair fell to his waist since he'd never cut it, but when he was working, he tied it back with a piece of leather. It was already tied back, so we just needed to set some boundaries so we didn't beat the shit out of each other. This was a friendly spar.

"No touching my hair and no hitting the face. If I pin you, you have to tell me what's really going on with you and Lance. I always knew I'd eventually learn to protect and care for these girls. You stepped up for all of them when your mom moved in. I get why you stepped away from us better than anyone. You could have come back when you were trained. You still could."

I grunted. I needed to let off some steam, but I definitely didn't want to spill my guts about Lance Argent. I guess I'd just have to win.

"If I pin you, we never talk about Lance Argent ever again."

Beck just smirked and my cock and I definitely paid attention to that. I had to calm down because I didn't want Beck to feel or see that. I definitely didn't need to catch feelings for yet another one of my friends. And Beck was definitely flirting with me because he winked.

"You know you just gave me extra motivation to get you underneath me?"

Definitely flirting. I rather liked it. Most people who flirted with me were utterly insane and I didn't particularly want them anywhere near my family. I just got vibes off of them they'd get clingy and probably kill Rowena's cat when I tried to get rid of them. Beck wasn't like that.

"I don't know. I'm pretty motivated to not discuss my feelings about Lance with anyone."

Beck gave a belly laugh, but then he exploded at me. We'd set the rule no damage to the face, but a good throat punch would end most fights. We both started learning when we got out of school. I hadn't hit my growth spurt yet and was pretty puny, so I was taught to go straight for the throat.

I grinned. Beck had clearly been taught that, too, and wanted to play. He knew I needed a good fight, but he also knew we'd be trained by the same man. I barely blocked him and got out of the way. I used his forward momentum to grab his arm, swing him towards me, and try to choke him out.

Fuck. Jagged Key Isles folks took these long-perfumed baths every day. He smelled really good. It was a combination of his natural musk with spices and a little vanilla. I heard Beck chuckle and while I was distracted by how good he smelled, he managed to jam his elbow up my ribcage and get away.

We faced each other with our fists raised. Beck was grinning like a psycho and I didn't need a mirror to know I was, too.

"Are you wearing perfume like the women?" I asked, throwing a fist at his gut.

I knew damned well about the perfumed baths. All the girls at the brothel had adopted the habit so they smelled good for the men. Rowena had gotten obsessed with them about a year ago, so I started buying her what she needed because I didn't want her raiding the brothel stash. It made her happy. I was mostly trying to get Beck talking so I could pin him.

I *really* didn't want to talk about Lance and if I lost and didn't fulfill the wager, Beck would never spar with me again.

He just laughed and danced away.

"Men of my culture take perfumed baths and wear scented oil. We carried that over with us when we came to Guttertown and introduced it. The rest of Nestran likes to pretend Guttertown is the unwashed masses, but I've been smelling the men who come in here since I was a child. We bathe much more often than the rest of Nestran," Beck said, trying to hook my knee with his foot.

I got a pretty good blow to his chest while he was distracted, but Beck was way too good at this. He could talk *and* beat a man's ass. Beck clipped my shoulder with his fist, so I danced away. I didn't think I'd had this much fun in a long time. Beck was grinning, too. We were pretty evenly matched because we were trained by the same man and I wasn't going to break out what Keeva taught me.

Beck broke rank and dove straight for my middle. I wasn't expecting it and went flying on my back with Beck on top of me. He had me pinned in an instant. The more I tried to buck him off, the more turned on I got.

I'd always been attracted to men. Lance was my first, but he wasn't the last. I'd never acted on my urges because my momma wanted grandbabies and Rowena wanted a nephew. I was attracted to women, too, so I just focused on them. The women who were attracted back to me were more unhinged than I was and that was a pretty hard thing to be.

Still, I was pinned beneath Beck and painfully erect. I definitely didn't want to talk about Lance. So, I snapped my head up and kissed Beck. It was my first kiss with a man.

And it was everything.

BECK

I thought everyone in our original group was into both men and women except Neco and Lance. Were we wrong about Lance, too? Because I thought Neco just kissed me because I bested him and he wanted to get out of talking about Lance. Then, he tangled his hands in my hair and really went for it.

Yeah, Neco was either *very* committed to not talking about Lance or he was into men. And you just didn't kiss like that if you weren't. My hand fumbled to his trousers, and he was rock hard. Yeah, definitely into this.

Neco let out a soft growl and ground his cock into my hand. I bit his neck.

"You could have kissed me when you weren't losing a fight."

Neco just laughed.

"I can't be into men."

I propped myself up on my elbow and started stroking his abs. Neco had nice abs.

"Why the fuck not? Half of Guttertown is. We don't agree with the nonsense the rest of Nestran believes."

"No, I agree with Guttertown. There's nothing wrong with it. But they did get something right. Momma wants grandbabies and Rowena wants a baby to play with. I can't do that with a man. And I like women."

"So do I. I like them a lot. Do you even want kids, Neco? Like, you? Not your mom and sister."

"Dunno. I haven't met a woman I wanted to have them with yet."

"Then what's stopping you from playing around until you met her? This is Guttertown. The woman you marry might want to play with other men *with* you. Remember Lissa from school? She used to play with Ollie, Ronan, and me. She married that blacksmith's apprentice who is into Ollie and they invite him to their bedroom all the time. Ollie only tells them no because he can't stand the apprentice."

"No shit?"

"Yeah. And your mom and Rowena adore you. They wouldn't care if you were *just* into men."

"I'm not. I *really* like women. Problem is, the only ones who like me are a little scary."

I laughed because if anyone had *any* sense, they'd be afraid of Neco. He was fiercely protective of his people, but he also decided every woman and child in Guttertown were his people. I don't think most people knew his secret, but you could just tell from looking at him that he could pop your head like a grape if he was in a bad mood.

I let my hand trail down to his cock. It was still hard.

"I'm attracted to you. I just always thought you weren't into men. *I'm* a little scary," I growled.

I slipped my hand down the front of his trousers and gripped his cock. Neco moaned when I started stroking it.

"You're not the same kind of scary and I can just hit you when you come at me. Men who hit women deserve to die."

Clearly, since if they did it in Guttertown, they were mysteriously ending up dead and a bag of gold was found by their victims. But Neco could tell me about that when he was ready. We'd just hit a breakthrough in our relationship and I wasn't about to ruin it.

I just knew Neco had never been with a man before because he put rules on himself. Even if we never did this again, and I hoped we did, Neco needed this. He was so focused on protecting his family, and his murder side hobby, he wasn't taking much time for himself. Unless that was what the murder side hobby was for, but that wasn't really healthy.

I untied the laces to his trousers and pulled them down. Fuck me. Neco was a giant with his clothes on and off. There was one thing the rest of Nestran didn't understand. Women knew what women liked in the bedroom and men knew what men liked. They all came here and paid for sex because we were open enough to compare notes. The girls at the brothel gave me pointers to please women, and I gave them some tips on giving head for their Johns.

They were tips I was about to get all over Neco's cock. I gripped the shaft and swirled the head with my tongue. I used my thumb to massage the spot between his balls and his arse before I took him down the back of my throat. Damn, he was big. And it was kind of a power trip having Guttertown's own serial killer at my mercy.

I didn't take it easy on Neco. I'd known Neco since we were toddlers. He didn't do easy, and he never shied away from anything difficult. I furiously bobbed my head on his cock while working him with my hand.

Neco just snarled. He tangled his hands in my hair and tried to move my head harder. I didn't mind. Ronan got a little enthusiastic sometimes. I briefly wondered if I'd ever find out how Lance liked his cock sucked. I mean, I didn't think

Neco was into men, either. The five us of in bed together as adults was something everyone but Neco and Lance wanted.

But this was about Neco, not anyone else. I wasn't going to give him a prostate massage with no oil, but a taint massage felt good, too. Neco growled and tried to push me away.

"Fuck! I'm going to cum."

Oh, that wasn't how this worked. I was just as strong as he was and refused to let him push me away. No, his orgasm was *mine.* I kept going until he spilled into my mouth. I sat back on my heels feeling immensely proud of myself.

"We can do that *any* time you want. If you're up for it, Ronan and Ollie would probably want to play, too. Even if you decide you ever want to talk to or about Lance, we'd like that, too. None of us can figure out if Lance is into men like that, but he's still a good friend."

Neco just grunted.

"My idea of pillow talk isn't discussing my mortal enemy. If you're going to bring up Lance after my dick was in your mouth, then we can't do this again. And I want to return the favor, so don't ruin it."

I sighed. Neco and Lance were both Argents, but in Guttertown, that just meant your father was one of ten Barons. They didn't look like they were remotely related. Neco was dark and huge while Lance was lithe and fair. We'd never know for sure until Lance found out who is father was and told us.

Lance and Neco Argent might not look alike, but they were both pig-headed stupid enough to be half siblings.

LUCY

Mom *always* beat me awake in the morning. Her not being up before me on a night she didn't close up the tavern was a bad sign because that literally never happened before. Maybe when I was a baby and crying all the time, but not since I started sleeping through the night and not as long as I could remember.

I was pretty sure it was related to whatever was making her cough. I had time before I had to check on my experiments and open the tavern with Ollie. We weren't starving like some of Guttertown. People liked to fuck and drink. They could drink here and go fuck or fuck and then come here. Mom did some clever bookkeeping, so the Barons thought we weren't doing as well as we were when it came to the taxes they levied on the tavern.

I went straight to the kitchen and started scrambling some eggs. She needed to keep her strength up. We usually had left-over bread from the tavern. We took half a loaf home every night and sold the rest. I smashed some garlic and spread it with some butter on the bread. I made some herbal tea and orange juice and brought it to her in bed.

Mom looked paler than usual. I put my hand on her forehead. Did she have a fever? I hadn't learned to check a temperature like a mom yet. She hissed and swatted my hand away.

"You know better than to wake the women in our family up and you're too old for a nightmare."

Yeah, I did know better and usually these roles were reversed.

"It's morning and I beat you awake. You need to eat and keep your strength up."

"What?" she shrieked, trying to sit up.

Mom got dizzy and started coughing again. I handed her the cup of tea. Ugh. I hated this. My mom was the strongest person I knew, and I hated seeing her like this. She saw how I was looking at her.

"Relax. It's going to take more than a cough to kill me."

I made the gesture to ward off evil. Mom loved doing that. She'd say something just to watch me freak out and make that gesture, but it existed for a reason. You could talk curses and bad luck into existence. I also made a rude gesture with my middle finger because she was laughing at me.

"Language, my only child," she said, gripping my finger.

"It wasn't a word, it was a gesture."

"It's still rude."

"*I'm* rude."

"Were you rude when you dropped the soup off for Theda?"

Ugh. Mom knew all. Even when she was upstairs all day, she knew what I was up to. I brought the soup to Theda, but hadn't mentioned I took some to Theda because I didn't want to talk about Neco. I usually told Mom everything, but she always found out when I didn't want to tell her something. She had this way of asking me without making me feel like a liar.

"Only to Neco, but he deserves it."

"You know he doesn't."

"Oh, he does. And he was rude right back."

Mom just sighed.

"Am I being grounded again?"

"Yes! You overslept. You clearly need the rest. Ollie and I will work the tavern. Ronan has been helping."

"And your experiment?"

"I'm still figuring out how long to infuse the mango. Two days is not enough. I think a week is perfect, but I want to add other things to it. The taste isn't perfect yet. Then, I have to make enough to stock the bar."

"What have you tried so far?"

"I've got three jars. One is just mango, one is mango and apricot, and I have another with mango, apple, and nutmeg. The last one is the one I have the most hope for."

"Focus on the last one. It's a little more nuanced. It could become the signature drink of the Whispering Raven."

"You think?"

"I know, my one and only."

"I also think I could do something with it plain with tomatoes and stuff we have in the kitchen to make a savory drink."

"That's because you're my child. Go. Be brilliant."

"Rest," I said, kissing the top of her head.

My jars still had a few days. I just needed to shake them. I poured a little of the plain spirits into a glass because I was pretty sure I could introduce it with what I had planned. We shared a courtyard with the brothel. There were mango trees and vegetables and fruit out there. We had an arrangement to share as long as we didn't take too much. The Whispering Raven and the brothel both cared for it.

I picked a few tomatoes and set to work. Ollie came in after I'd smashed them in the mortar and pestle. He found me squeezing them through a cheese cloth into a glass. That beautiful face looked at me like I was utterly insane. Ronan came in right behind him. I knew both of them were about to give me all kinds of shit about this.

"That's fucked up Lance," Ollie said. "I know tomatoes are technically a fruit, but it's not the same as orange juice."

"Did you just wake up this morning and choose to drink a tomato?"

"It's not weird! Tomato soup is a thing."

"Yeah, but it's fundamentally different. It's not fucked up when you're eating it hot from a bowl with a spoon when it's got spices in it. You look like you're about to chug it plain from a tankard. It's not right. Did you catch a bedroom disease that messes with your mind? The healers can fix that, you know."

"Dick," I said, throwing a bar cloth at his face. "The new spirit I'm working on is pretty versatile. I'm still trying to figure out the sweet option, but I had this idea when I was making soup last night."

"You're going to make us drink it, aren't you?" Ronan moaned.

"Weren't you *just* saying the other day that you're my official taste testers?" I asked, squeezing a lemon into the glass.

"That was before you lost your fucking mind," Ollie said.

Guttertown had a sauce made from vinegar and anchovies. I added a few dashes with a little horseradish. Ollie and Ronan looked like they were about to faint. I tossed in some salt and pepper and gave it a stir.

I trusted Ollie and Ronan, but I also trusted myself. I sampled my creations first. I would have done it even if they weren't looking at me like I was asking them to drink piss. It was good. It was savory, and I knew the spirits would get people nice and drunk.

"Drink up or you're banished from being my taste testers. And I'll tell Mom you aren't allowed to be hers, either."

Ollie snatched the glass and glared at me.

"Rude."

Ollie looked like I was about to ruin his fucking life, but he wasn't about to lose his taste testing rights. It was one thing to lose them from me, but Mom was a much better cook than I was and you never wanted *her* to take them away. She liked Ollie and Ronan, but she was in labor for ten hours with me. She'd always side with me in public and call me out in private if she didn't agree with me.

Ollie downed half of it in one go, set the tankard on the bar, and had to think about it for a minute.

"Okay, so I'm man enough to admit when I'm wrong. That's delicious and I'm feeling the spirits with just half the tankard. If we can actually get people to put alcoholic tomato juice in their mouth, this would take off. But you have to admit, Lance, that it's fucking weird."

"Seriously?" Ronan said, draining the rest of the tankard. "Okay, so yeah, that's great, and it hits you pretty hard, even with just a little bit of it. But it's going to be a weird sell. It's either going to need a badass name or you're going to have to say it's soup that fucks you up."

"You're the creative one. Get creative because I'd just go with alcoholic soup," Ollie said.

"My forte is creating, not naming. This one is all you, buddy. Make it good."

"Guttertown doesn't have fancy books, but we do like our oral stories. The legends about the knights rescuing the damsels don't hit the same in Guttertown. Our women save themselves for the most part and we all know if the knight showed up here, he'd just shit on us like the rest of Nestran.

"No, we need a good old-fashioned Guttertown legend. The one *every* child knows. The woman in the mirror. She's supposed to come if you say her name three times in the dark. You give her a name and she'll go to a mirror in that person's house and brutally murder them for you. Guttertown justice. The drink is red like blood. It can *only* be called a Bloody

Mary. *That's* the name that's going to get Guttertown to take a chance on it."

We'd all stood in front of the mirror and tried to call Bloody Mary down on someone. The night everything exploded with Neco, I started my period, and found out I was really a girl with the worst possible Baron as a father, I tried for five straight nights to summon her to kill Folcard. Oddly, I never wanted to send her after Neco. I hated him but I didn't want him dead.

There was magic in Nestran. People could set things on fire with their minds or shift into animals. People like the Barons had been trying to control and steal that magic for a long time. We were just trying to survive in Guttertown and eventually realized there was no magic mirror woman coming to save us.

But still, everyone in Guttertown knew and feared her at one point and I had made a very red drink.

"It's *perfect,*" I said.

"Do you have enough of your spirits to make this drink tonight?" Ollie asked.

"I'm calling it vodka and no. I've been working on the spirit for a while. It doesn't need to be aged in a barrel, but I'm seeing if it gives it unique qualities if I do. I've got seven barrels of it I can't open yet and one that I already have is being used to figure out the infused recipe."

"How long?" Ollie asked. "The Bloody Mary could bring in a lot of money once it catches on. Some of the people who buy spirits when they should be buying food would buy it because it's not just empty calories like ale and the people who buy both would drink it because it's delicious and pretty fucking strong."

"We can open two of the barrels to start serving it, but we're going to have to figure out an easy way to make the base."

"Then, we need to start planning. The Madame loves

tomatoes and if you use all the ones in the courtyard, she's probably going to send some of her scarier relatives after us. My uncle will probably let us rent a plot on his farm to grow tomatoes and what we need for your spirits. If we use his workers to tend to our crops, we're going to have to chip in to pay them.

"That'll solve the supply issue, but we can't crush and strain tomatoes for every drink, so we'll have to make that part beforehand. You also need to teach me the recipe since I'm the one slinging drinks. Leave talking it up to me. By the time it's ready to debut, people will have been asking for it for weeks."

Yeah, I believed that. Ollie wasn't just beautiful. He had a silver tongue. I was *shocked* I hadn't spilled my guts to him that I wasn't a boy because everyone else told them their secrets and he always repeated them to me. Which was why I never told him I was a girl like Mom constantly told me I should do.

First things first. Ollie was a wonderful cook once he mastered a recipe, but he usually fucked up several times before he got it right. That probably should have annoyed the shit out of me since we were running a business, but Ollie was Ollie. He could nearly burn the tavern down and you'd think it was adorable.

It was very annoying because I knew I should have been pissed.

"Gather round because you're about to learn how to make a Bloody Mary," I said with flourish.

RONAN

We had a lot of fun learning to make the Bloody Marys. A few of the regulars came in. The ones that started drinking pretty early in the morning. They were very curious as to what we were doing. Lance and Ollie had a much better head for business than I did. I was better at slinging ale.

"What's that you've got there?" Old Man Aimes asked.

Ollie swooped in and turned on the Ollie charm.

"It's a new drink Lance worked up. It's called a Bloody Mary."

"That actual blood?"

Ollie slid the tankard over.

"Not at all, but it'll get you drunker faster than anything here. Want to be our first customer taste tester? It's on the house."

Old Man Aimes was a harmless drunk. He was one of the older Argent kids. His father pulled him into his army and after his body had been broken, had no use for him. It was one of the *many* reasons we hated the Barons. Guttertown usually took care of him, even if most of us also didn't have a lot.

"Let me get you some stew first," Lance said. "It's pretty bloody strong."

Lance wasn't going to charge him for the stew. He was usually the first person in the Whispering Raven when it opened. They didn't usually charge him unless there were other customers and when they did, it was usually barter. Old Man Aimes's eyes were sparkling.

"You ain't trying to poison me, are ye?"

"Never. You're my favorite customer," Ollie said.

Lance came back with stew and a piece of bread.

"You might want to get some of that in your stomach before you try the drink."

Aimes was rail thin and we could hear his stomach growling when he walked in. He hadn't been in since I started taking a few shifts here, but he did that sometimes. He'd disappear for a bit and turn up, eventually. Aimes had been doing that since we were little.

"You're good kids," Aimes said.

Lance had overfilled his bowl of soup and given him a bigger piece of bread. Aimes was always a little thinner when he was missing. He was probably going to outlive everyone out of spite.

"Where were you this time, Aimes?" Ollie asked.

Aimes walked with a limp and he was half drunk the majority of the time. He was one of the oldest people in Guttertown, but that never stopped him. He wasn't sleeping it off in a piss-filled ditch when he disappeared. Aimes had the same education the rest of Guttertown did, but instead of learning a trade when he got out of school, his father had him cracking heads until he damaged his leg and couldn't learn most trades in Guttertown.

Still, the reason everyone was willing to barter with him

and hire him for odd jobs was because of *what* he got up to when he disappeared. As a former Baron's general, he knew his way around every part of Nestran. He also had respect outside of Guttertown.

Aimes would disappear for a few days and come back with gossip, trade agreements, or some kind of seeds that would help us. It took him a while because he walked and had to take frequent breaks.

"On an adventure, like always. I've been trying to find proof it was the Barons who took the Princess Lisana. They went hard for the shifters, but they never had any motive. The Barons do. They've been trying to breed the Tempris line out of existence and they nearly have. Kidnapping the heir and blaming the shifters is a good way to wipe out any lingering fire magic, seize the throne, and start another war. They've been itching for that since they made me their general."

Only fuckers who weren't going to be fighting and dying in it wanted war. They were happy for the rest of us to die in it, though. We didn't intentionally go into the shifters' lands and they didn't come into ours, but sometimes, we'd meet each other in the space between.

If you made it clear you meant them no harm, they didn't mean you any, either. Which said a lot because the Barons had them kidnapped and tortured for a long time. They knew we weren't all bad, so most of us knew they weren't. Sometimes, we helped each other and then went home and never spoke about it.

No one wanted the Tempris line off the throne except the Barons. King Joron kept them from being completely unreasonable, even if he was mostly powerless. The Barons were dumbasses sometimes, even with their fancy education. The only people who believed their lies were their sycophants.

"Did you find anything?" Lance asked.

None of us would ever lay eyes on the Princess Lisana. Her mother was supposed to be the most beautiful woman in

Nestran. Guttertown would just have to take everyone's word for that because we'd never get close enough to the royal family to see any of them. The Barons had zero respect for women but the missing princess was still a better option than the Barons running things unchecked.

"No. But I did pick up something interesting. Someone is picking off wealthy men in Nestran. The Barons think it's the same man, but Inspector Trevils, Leodos, and myself think we are dealing with two different killers."

"What? Really?" Ollie asked. "Trevils was in here the other day. He just mentioned one they are calling The Blight. If anyone asks, the Blight practiced in Guttertown, but they aren't from here."

We just nodded. Ollie only repeated secrets if they were harmless and he only ever told them to us because he knew we weren't going to spread it around. If Ollie was protecting a murderer, he probably had a damned good reason.

"Trevils is brilliant. He's never going to discuss his theories outside of people he trusts until he's totally sure. Leodos and I are inner circle. Trevils hates the Barons just as much as Guttertown does. He *always* pinpoints the culprit, but he has to give the name to the Barons to do something about it. The Barons don't always send the guard after the right person if it doesn't fit their agenda. He's sick of it."

"What do you know?" Ollie asked.

Ollie seemed really invested in this and he'd better spill later.

"It's definitely two killers. One is meticulous. He's breaking into houses and killing the man of the house without tipping his family off. He's not leaving any evidence, and he's not taking anything. The other is brutal and messy. He's slaughtering everyone in the house, trashing it, and he's stealing a family heirloom as a trophy. The second one is also leaving bloody boot prints all over the place."

"Fuck," Lance said. "They are going to try to pin this on us, aren't they?"

"Not the messy one. They haven't narrowed down the cobbler, but they are expensive boots. The messy one isn't from Guttertown. He's brutal, and he's not sparing the women or children, but it's the other one that's got Trevils and Leodos worried. There's no evidence and no motive they can find. No one they talked to can think of why they were targeted."

I'd bet my left nut fucking Ollie knew why. He might not know who the butcher was, but if he was covering for one of the murderers, he knew exactly who they were and why they were doing this. And he thought their motive was a good one.

"Anyway, that's the drama outside of Guttertown. Trevils is a sly dog, and he hates most everyone. Leodos is helping him, but you know how Leodos feels about Guttertown."

Guttertown felt the same about Leodos. He was the *only* Baron we liked, and that was because he wasn't a Baron anymore. His family used to experiment on the shifters to find out how to steal their magic. Leodos told them to get fucked and burned their research so they couldn't continue.

He was his father's only son, but Leodos was disinherited and banished to Guttertown with no money. The previous Madame hired him to protect the girls and manage her books, but he didn't stop there. Nah, Leodos went around teaching all the Guttertown businesses to fix their books for when the Barons sent someone to look at them so they could figure out if they wanted to raise taxes because they thought we could afford it.

Yeah, Leodos got called back to the palace to be King Joron's advisor. The Barons hated it and Guttertown missed him, but he left behind a hefty legacy of tax evasion because fuck the Barons.

"The stew was excellent as always. I'm a little suspicious of your new beverage."

"Don't be," I said. "It's delicious and the spirit in it is something Lance has been working on. It's *very* strong."

"Come on, Aimes," Ollie said with that smile no one could resist. "Have you *ever* eaten or drunk anything bad in this tavern?"

"Good point," Aimes said.

And with that, he basically guzzled the whole Bloody Mary. Lance and Caitrin would have been gifted alchemists with the right education, but this was Guttertown, so their experiments involved ale and spirits. Lance's last batch hit hard, and that was just me finishing half the tankard Ollie didn't finish.

I think all three of us had our eyes bugging out of our head, but if anyone could handle what was probably Lance's strongest experiment to date, it was Old Man Aimes. He slammed the tankard on the table and whistled.

"Fuck! That is potent. This is going to put the Whispering Raven on the map."

If Old Man Aimes endorsed your booze, that meant everyone in Guttertown was going to love it.

What the fuck were we going to do about the competing serial killers and how did Ollie know one of them?

LUCY

Some of my experiments were utter failures that couldn't be salvaged. I used to get upset about that, but Mom said it happened to her, too. I knew the Bloody Mary idea was weird. Guttertown didn't have anything like it. The people in our tavern drank ale or whiskey straight.

It was a risk, but Mom took those all the time. If I wanted to be totally self-reliant and never have my father find out about me, I had to take them, even if it might be weird and new. I needed to ramp it up because of Mom's cough because she might need the best healers.

Guttertown had skilled healers, but they didn't have access to the same equipment. They needed copper equipment to make certain remedies, and that was impossible. Folcard controlled the largest copper ore in Nestran that we knew of. The shifters might have some of their lands, but we weren't welcome there.

Folcard who controlled who got that copper and what the prices were. Guttertown couldn't afford it and even if we could, he wouldn't have sold it to us. They weren't actively trying to wipe us out like they were the shifters, but they didn't give a shit if we lived or died.

But I had a good start at hiring a healer that did have access to copper equipment. I couldn't get a healer that was working for a Baron unless I made myself known to my father, but I *could* get a healer who didn't.

I needed to get to the basement and get some barrels started so we could start serving Bloody Marys. The mango recipe wasn't done yet, and I still needed my test barrel to see if aging it did anything, but I knew it was fine without it.

But first things first. Ollie and his fucking secrets.

Ollie knew something about the murders or he wouldn't have told us to lie. People died in Guttertown all the time and sometimes violently. But I'd remember if either scenario happened here. I got more of the Guttertown gossip train because I lived and worked in a tavern and if I didn't personally hear it, Ollie told me.

As soon as Aimes left and we were alone again for a few minutes, I turned to Ollie.

"Fess up, Ollie. No one was murdered like that in Guttertown. Why did *you* lie to Trevils and why are you asking the rest of us to?"

Because Old Man Aimes had been coming in the Whispering Raven since I was a kid. I'd always loved his stories. Mom had been giving him food and drink in exchange for odd jobs. One of those odd jobs used to be watching me and keeping me out of trouble when I was too young and stupid to do that myself.

Leodos came to the Whispering Raven a lot. I'd met him several times. The man lived in the palace with the king and the princess, but he said no one did whiskey like my mom. He only bought his from us and if Mom had any questions about her books, he'd help. The man was insanely tall, but I liked him.

Aimes had been telling me stories of the famous Inspector

Trevils since he was my drunk babysitter. He was wicked smart. He'd piece things together with seemingly minor details. It was almost like magic. It was probably really fucking stupid for Ollie to lie to him.

"Okay, get close," Ollie said. "This is the first I'm hearing about a second killer, but Trevils was in here asking about one killer they were calling The Blight. I don't know anything about the second killer because I haven't heard anything. I know the motive of the one not leaving any evidence."

It had better be a fucking good one because if Trevils found out Ollie lied for a killer, this wasn't going to be a night in the cells for him. Ollie would hang for that if the Barons decided he should. At most, he'd die in the cells.

"Then why did you lie instead of telling Trevils that?" Ronan said.

Thank you! Ollie wasn't stupid most of the time. I mean, yeah, there were a solid few years where Ollie's ideas landed us in the cells for the night and Mom was furious with me, but sixteen-year-old boys did stupid shit and so did sixteen-year-old girls pretending to be boys.

"The men who have been dying with no evidence have a connection to Guttertown. They all hurt someone here. Like, in a way that would matter if it happened outside of Guttertown, but since it didn't, nothing was going to happen to them. Someone made sure it did."

"There are several ways to hurt someone, Ollie. You need to be specific."

We didn't have much, but it was possible to fuck up someone's livelihood and leave them with nothing at all. They could come to Guttertown and lay their hands on whoever they wanted. If we fought back, they'd just lie and say we attacked them unprovoked. All of Guttertown could show up as witnesses that it didn't go down like that and it wouldn't fucking matter.

"They are beating the shit out of people. Mostly women,

but some of them have kicked some kids that were in their way. The rest of Nestran has some pretty shit ideas about beating your own wife and kids, but it's different when it's not your wife and those aren't your kids.

"Except if they are Guttertown women and kids, you can do whatever you want to them. Someone is getting justice for Guttertown and the rest of Guttertown would have my back lying for them. You two just have to get on board."

You had to be a little morally gray to survive in Guttertown, but a line had to be drawn somewhere. Like, Mom taught me to cheat our taxes by the time I was thirteen and then she taught Ollie. Still that was business and the Barons weren't using the tax money to better anything like they were supposed to.

But was I mad someone was murdering people for hurting us here in Guttertown? It wasn't like there was a justice system for us. Well, there was if *we* hurt each other. But not if *they* hurt us. They could do whatever they wanted to us.

I mean, whoever was doing this, good for them.

Ronan was looking at me expectantly because I knew I was the holdout. Ronan would be fine with this. Honestly? So was I.

"We can use the tavern to spread the word."

Because I wasn't protecting this killer anymore. Ollie lied for him. I needed to protect Ollie. I couldn't lose him. Ollie would protect Mom and me by saying we didn't know, but we had each other's back here. I knew Guttertown felt the same. If everyone knew one of our own was protecting us, they'd protect him.

"Who is it?" Ronan asked.

"I can't say. For his protection and yours."

I nodded. I got it. No one could know. Most people wouldn't say anything, but not everyone in Guttertown would keep that secret if money was involved. I mean, most of us would take the gold and lie to anyone's face, but not everyone.

It was probably fucking stupid to get the tavern tangled up in this and Mom would kill me, but I thought it was a good cause. Some of those men had probably come into the tavern and made a mess. They probably had it coming.

Ronan was going to keep digging. He did that. I wasn't going to seek out who was doing it for my protection and Mom's, but I wasn't going to complain if that information fell into my lap. Ronan was going to be like a dog with a bone until he found out.

Hopefully, Ollie had the sense to protect him and not tell him.

OLIVER

Would I have done things differently if Trevils had given me his name before I lied to his face? Some of the adults didn't pay attention to Old Man Aimes's drunken stories and didn't particularly care where he disappeared to, but the kids all *loved* his stories. I'd never met Trevils before, but Aimes had told us stories about him.

Yeah, you know what? I still would have lied. Neco might have pulled away from us, but I still loved him and would protect him like he was protecting the rest of Guttertown.

Ronan would ask, but I was hoping Lance wouldn't. Lance was usually calculating and reasonable until he wasn't. Sometimes, he would just fly off and want to hit someone. Most of those situations involved Neco Argent. Neco hated Lance back just as strongly, but I didn't think Lance hated him enough for him to hang.

Thankfully, Lance didn't want to know. He was just satisfied with my reason why I protected a killer. He didn't need to know the name, and I was glad because I made it a point not to lie to my friends when they asked me a question.

"Do you think you can handle the tavern?" Lance asked.

"I *know* the vodka is fine without aging, I'm just experimenting to see what happens when it does. I don't have the recipe right for the infused version, but I *can* get production started so we can start serving Bloody Marys. I just need to convince our fucking donkey to bring the cart to Ollie's uncle's because I need to buy lots of potatoes."

I tried not to laugh because Lance *would* hit me. Lance was probably feuding with that donkey harder than he was with Neco. The donkey probably hated Lance as much as Neco did, but she also hated everyone but me. Caitrin bought her at a steep discount because no one else wanted her. Guttertown had no problem eating horse meat in a pinch, but I guess we all drew the line at donkeys.

People were weird sometimes.

Last time Lance tried to convince the donkey to do something she didn't want to do, Lance got the shit kicked out of him and it took him two months to heal. I couldn't do much to run interference when Lance and Neco got heated, but women loved me. Apparently, female donkeys also loved me.

Who was I to question the gods?

"Um, we need you making vodka, not recovering because you got the shit kicked out of you by an angry donkey. I'll handle Petunia."

"Naming that demon beast Petunia was false advertising. If you name a donkey Petunia, she should be sweet and docile," Lance muttered.

"That donkey is sweet as pie if you're me," I bragged.

Yeah, I was probably asking to get hit. Lance was about as sensitive about the donkey as he was about Neco Argent.

"Go do your magic with the demon donkey because I don't really want to be out of commission because she kicked me, either. That shit hurts."

Petunia hated the bridle and cart and everything it stood for. You couldn't just walk up to her and put it on her. You had to sweet talk her, give her presents, and make it nice. It was a lot like anal sex. If you skipped the prep work, you were probably going to get your arse kicked.

I grabbed a carrot on my way out because they were Petunia's favorite. She tossed her head and looked excited to see me because I always bought treats. I offered her the carrot and scratched her neck.

"Hey, you big sexy beast. How do you feel about making the trip to my uncle's farm? You'll get to see his stallions and I know you're crushing on Damek. Who knows? Maybe one day, you'll get utterly railed by a giant, spotted stallion. I'm rooting for you."

Petunia was a pervert. If you gave her carrots and the possibility of stallion sex, she'd happily get hitched to the cart. Lance didn't believe me, but I'll bet if he tried that, Petunia wouldn't constantly try to kick the shit out of him.

Sometimes, I thought Lance didn't understand women at all.

Petunia stepped out of her pen and made herself ready for me to hitch the cart. Easy. Lance came out and rolled his eyes.

"I swear, I don't know how you do that."

"You have to be nice to women if you want them to do something. You need to learn women if you want to snag a good wife."

Lance just rolled his eyes and walked away. I went back into the tavern and Ronan was washing glasses.

"Spill," he said.

"You can't tell Lance."

"Since when do we keep secrets?"

"It's fucking Neco. At least, Beck and I are pretty sure of it. Every time a girl gets beaten at the brothel, a bag of gold gets slipped into her room, and eventually I hear about someone getting their throat slit. We compared notes. They don't give their names, but they usually say what their trade is. They match up. Neco lives in the brothel and he has the same training Beck does. He said Neco is the only one who could sneak around."

"Or, if he can break into a house and slit a man's throat without waking up his family, he could easily break into the brothel and give money to the girls. I thought nothing was stolen?"

"You know people with money keep some hidden. I don't even have money and I have some hidden," I said.

"Good point. It might not be Neco, though."

"How would he know those particular girls had hands laid on them?" I asked.

"A John?"

"Maybe. Shit, how do we ask Neco if this is him without setting him off?"

I didn't particularly want to have that conversation with Neco. We needed Beck for this.

"We're going to the brothel after the tavern closes."

LUCY

Maybe it should say something about me that my nemesis were a mountain of a man with one eye and a donkey. Or you could just say they were both asses. I liked that better. Mom bought Petunia when I was thirteen and that fucking donkey had hated me ever since. If she wasn't trying to kick me, she was biting.

I gave Ollie a hard time about his connection with our idiot donkey, but I was grateful he could get her pulling the cart. I managed to get the potatoes bought. I didn't haggle much with Ollie's uncle because he was a good man who needed the money. I also didn't buy all his potatoes because he needed some of them. We came to a fair price.

I managed to get Petunia back home and in her pen. She only tried to bite me and kick me twice. Fucking ass. Ronan came out to help me load everything into the basement. The tavern was starting to get busy because people were getting off of work.

When I went upstairs to check on Mom, she was taking a nap. She had a handkerchief in her hand and that was when I saw it. She had been coughing up blood. That did it. I was getting a healer in here tomorrow. I'd start with a Guttertown healer first. I wasn't going to wake her.

Ollie and Ronan had the tavern covered. I snuck out the back and caught Athan on his way out the door. He was Ilyn's brother. Their sister was also a healer. Athan agreed to bring Tarja tomorrow if I paid them both. Mom would be pissed, but she was just going to have to deal with the expense. I wasn't going to lose her. She'd do the same if it were me and she fucking knew that.

I tried to run all the way back to the tavern because I really needed to get that vodka started if I was bringing in healers. I'd start with Guttertown and if that didn't work, I'd ask Aimes to use his connections to get me another one.

Everyone was getting off of work. They were hitting up the market for dinner, going to the brothel, or headed to my tavern. I was dodging bodies left and right, but in dodging one, I ran face first into a giant with a hard chest. I hoped it wasn't Neco. I wasn't a short person, but I only knew a few people that much taller than me.

The person grabbed me so I didn't end up on my ass in the dirt. When I looked up, it was Leodos, not Neco.

"If you're running from the law, I don't want to know," he said.

Leodos wasn't from Guttertown, but he was decent like that.

"Running home. Mom's sick. Hey, if I have to get a healer outside of Guttertown, do you think you could get me the same one the king and princess use? I might be able to pay for it if my experiments pay off."

Because that would solve everything with my father for now. I might need him again, but not any time soon.

"Let me see what I can do. It'll have to be in secret or everyone will want their healer. Joron and Esylle are great and I'm pretty sure they'd want to loan out their healer, but they can't be seen playing favorites and they don't know you. What experiments?"

"I've got one called a Bloody Mary that we're going to be serving soon. Come by and I'll let you try one on the house. I've also got a new spirit that I'm experimenting with infusing fruit in it."

"You know I'm never going to let you give me a drink for free. I told Caitrin the same."

"Might as well since you taught us how to cheat on our taxes."

Leodos ruffled my hair. If my father had to be any Baron, I wished it was Leodos. I was pretty sure he was desperately in love with the Princess Esylle based on how he talked about her. I'd never say that to him, though. His secrets were his own.

"I taught you all how to survive the ruling class."

"Same thing. Gotta go," I said, zipping away again.

"Watch where you're going this time!" Leodos called.

The next time I ran into someone, it wasn't super great. It was another giant, and it happened to be Neco. As soon as he realized it was me, he shoved me into the dirt. He stood over me clenching his fists.

"Are you *trying* to start shit with me, Lance?"

"First of all, fuck you. I'm trying to get home to take care of my mom. She's got the same cough Theda does."

Neco narrowed his eyes at me and offered his hand to help me up.

"The soup changes nothing, but thank you."

Ugh. I swatted his hand away and got to my feet.

"I didn't make it to change anything. I made it because I like your mom and sister. And fuck you again, but if she needs anything, we'll be here for her. Just send Rowena," I said, stomping off.

My arse was killing me because Neco shoved me pretty hard. Dick. I needed to spend the rest of the night making vodka. I had enough squirrelled away to pay the healers tomorrow, but if I needed another one, I'd need more money. I knew it was an enormous risk asking Leodos, but I got this far taking risks.

I had potatoes and a healer. I was pretty set to work for the rest of the night.

NECO

Why was I *constantly* running into Lance Argent? All I was trying to do was get home from Ilyn's shop. Momma saw his brother Athan earlier in the day because I made her. I had the money because I stole it from the man I murdered. I didn't spend it as soon as we got it. I usually hid some.

I was going to buy us a house one day so she could retire from the brothel. I just wasn't there yet. One day. Right now, I'd happily spend money on the healers because she was coughing up blood.

Athan thumped all over her and confirmed she had an infection in her lungs. It wasn't the Pale Plague, so thank fuck for that. She quarantined herself at first because that was the Madame's rules. Athan said that was why Rowena and I didn't get it.

There were herbs he could prescribe that would lessen the cough, but if the infection got worse, I'd have to contact my father because the Barons had access to a compound that would help.

Mother fuck. I should have told Lance. His mom was sick,

too, and I had nothing against Caitrin. Lance was already tearing ass down the street back to the tavern. I needed to get to Ilyn's shop, but then I'd swing by the tavern just in case they hadn't gotten a healer yet.

Ilyn was a grumpy fuck on a good day, but he was pleasant as long as you didn't come into his shop covered in blood and gore or weren't snotting everywhere. And if you didn't show up five minutes before he was trying to close up like I did. Ilyn got less pissed about staying late than he did about blood and snot, so he helped me instead of kicking me out.

I had herbs and roots for Momma. I hated Lance, but I'd always liked and admired Caitrin. She offered Momma a job more than once, but we lost our house, too. The brothel had free room and board for her and two kids, so she never took Caitrin up on it.

I didn't know if Caitrin's cough was the same as what my mother had, but I could at least pass it on. That meant talking to Lance if I couldn't find Caitrin. Caitrin probably wouldn't be working. Lance wouldn't let her.

Lance just pissed me off. Every time I saw him, I remembered him kicking me when I was down and I wanted to hit him again. And then I realized how beautiful he was and that he was my first crush. I wanted to kiss him and that pissed me off, too, because I didn't know if we were half-brothers or not.

Ugh. And no one had been acting up in Guttertown, so I couldn't go slit a throat to make myself feel better. Though, I did really enjoy myself with Beck. I could do that again.

Best get this out of the way. I went straight to the Whispering Raven instead of the brothel. Ollie was behind the bar and Ronan was bussing tables, but Lance was nowhere to be found. Ollie knew everyone's business, so he'd know where Lance was.

I took a seat at the bar. Ollie also knew most of *my* business, including what I usually drank. He had a whiskey poured and slid it over to me before my ass was even on the stool.

"How's Theda? Did the soup help?"

"Athan saw her. He said it's some kind of lung infection. It could clear up with the herbs he recommended or it could get worse and I'd have to contact my father."

"Fuck. I don't know, man. That's rough. Lance knows that's a possibility, and he's been busting his ass coming up with new spirits to sell so he never has to."

I didn't particularly want to see my old man, either. I knew who he was, but I wasn't exactly throwing his name around Guttertown. I didn't want to be associated with that. He was a complete fuck-wit deadbeat with two kids he wasn't taking care of and if we ever needed anything from him, he'd demand payback.

"Lance might have to. Athan said there's a compound that would cure it, but only the Baron's healers can make it. He gave me a list of herbs and roots. I don't know if Caitrin has the same thing, but can you pass that along to Lance?"

I knew he would. Ollie loved talking. Always had for as long as I'd known him. He knew this was important, and he cared for Caitrin.

"Yeah, but I wish you and Lance would make peace and you could tell each other this shit. Lance was wrong for what he said to you, but he was a stupid kid acting out because his friend was cutting him out. Back then, Lance was always shooting his mouth off and doing stupid shit. He should have gotten his nose broken a lot more often, but he had us."

I grunted. I didn't want to talk about Lance.

"Lance did us a solid bringing the soup over. I hold no malice towards Caitrin. She's a good woman. I was returning the favor."

"Then consider this a favor. You have competition in the Trulos District," Ollie said, leaning in where no one could hear him.

What the fuck? Ollie knew everything about everyone, but there was no fucking way he could have known about my trips to the Trulos District. The very first thing Keeva taught me was how to travel in the shadows without being seen. No one could have seen me.

I just stared at Ollie. I really didn't want to slit his throat because he knew my secret. Ollie was goofy, and we'd played together since we were toddlers.

"Speak," I growled in a low voice.

"Beck and I pieced it together between what he knew from the brothel and what I overheard at the tavern. We don't give a shit. We think you're doing a great thing and will protect you. They've given you a nickname and there was an inspector in here asking questions. I *think* I put him off looking at Guttertown for suspects.

"But there's someone else killing in the Trulos district and I don't think they have the same reasons as you. They are also messy about it and killing the entire family, not just the men. They are leaving evidence everywhere and taking trophies like a sicko."

"The women and children, too?"

Because if he was, he'd find himself on the other end of my blade. All this recent interaction with Lance had put me on edge, but I couldn't kill anyone who didn't deserve it.

"Apparently. And before you get stabby about it, there's a pretty famous inspector looking into it and I didn't risk my beautiful arse lying to him so you could do something stupid and lose your head."

Ollie really did have a nice arse.

"I slice, not stab. And do you really want this man eventually making his way to Guttertown because he wasn't caught in time? Also, the Barons decide who faces justice. If this person is important, they might look the other way if he makes Guttertown his hunting ground.

"There's a difference between a serial killer and an assassin. You don't have to worry about me unless you earn my knife. This man is random and unpredictable. He's even more dangerous when you know the Barons may look the other way as long as it doesn't happen in their backyard."

"Be careful, Neco. You're still one of us and we care about you. If someone finds you at the scene struggling with the killer, they won't care what the truth is. You're from Guttertown and they will automatically pin it on you."

That much was true. Surprising another killer wasn't going to be like popping out of the shadows and slitting the throat of a man who thought he was safe in his sitting room. There would be a struggle and they would definitely pin it on me if they caught me.

My accent would give me away as being from Guttertown. It was the one thing I struggled with. Keeva said if I wanted to kill in the Trulos District, I needed to talk like them. I felt like a fancy-pants cunt every time I talked with that accent and could never pull it off because Keeva said I looked like I was sucking a lemon and trying to pass a really hard turd at the same time.

Yeah, Keeva was mean sometimes. She hurt my feelings, and I wasn't sure I had any sometimes.

I needed to practice the accent with a straight face. It would help me blend in if anyone talked to me and I could root out who this person was. I didn't *have* to surprise them at a kill scene. I'd only do that if the women and children were in danger.

This man liked to break into people's houses and kill them, but he wasn't as good at that as I was. Let's see how he liked it right before he died.

But first things first because I was curious.

"What nickname did they give me?"

OLIVER

Why were all my childhood friends so hot? Neco and Lance were the only ones from our original group that I hadn't experimented with sexually. Lance was complicated. He rocked that girl's entire world when we lost our virginity, but if he was dating a woman, he was doing it in secret. I heard all. I'd know about it. If he was dating a man, I'd know about it, too. Sometimes, he felt like Caitrin was encouraging him to be with me, but Lance always shut that down before it got interesting.

And then there was Neco. When he talked about swooping into the Trulos District and killing that menace it was totally swoon worthy. That should have scared me, but sometimes, I didn't have any sense.

"What nickname did they give me?"

He seemed really curious about his serial-killer name, but he also took offense at being lumped in with the other serial killer. I guess there was a difference? He called himself an assassin but didn't those people usually kill for money? Neco was doing it for free. Didn't that make him a serial killer? This was complicated.

"The Blight, but I don't know if they were talking about you or the other guy. Trevils asked about the Blight and mentioned your kills. I found out about the other guy after getting Lance's new spirit into Aimes."

Neco slammed his glass on the bar and I immediately poured him another whiskey. I figured if he got a little homicidal about his nickname, I could fight him off easier if he was a little lubricated.

"I can't decide if I like it or not. A blight would fuck up an entire realm, but it kills indiscriminately. I've got a fucking code. Should I try to correct this?"

Yeah, between Lance and Caitrin, the whiskey in the Whispering Raven would fuck you up fast. I didn't need Neco getting drunk and running his mouth about his serial killer nickname because I lied for him to Inspector Trevils.

"Maybe not, big guy. You're much scarier when you're an unknown menace creeping into merchant's houses and slitting their throats."

"Does *everyone* know?"

By everyone, I knew he meant Lance. Neco and Ronan had made their peace and Neco knew Ronan would keep his secret. Lance, even I wasn't sure about Lance. Lance and Neco used to be the closest out of all of us, but the hatred they held for each other now wasn't healthy.

"You could have asked directly, but no, he doesn't. He's not asking around, either. Lance was here when Aimes was talking about it. I don't know much about what you get up to when you leave Guttertown, but Beck said those girls are getting money and the men are ending up dead. That was enough for Beck and me and it's apparently enough for Lance. Lance agreed to protect you and doesn't want to know who is doing it. Ronan asked, but you know Ronan."

Ronan never *repeated* gossip, but he wanted all the tea. Since we couldn't afford books in Guttertown, we traded in tall tales, fables, and usually a *lot* of gossip. I heard a lot of it at the bar. I usually told it to my friends because Ronan wanted to hear it, but I also knew it would never leave the room.

"Hey, you really lied for me when you knew what I was doing?" Neco asked.

"Fuck, yes. You might have pulled away, but you'll always be one of us. I agree with what you're doing. Lance and Ronan do, too. The rest of Guttertown would as well. I'm working on something to get them to back up my lie so they don't come sniffing back here. That just leaves you being careful when you leave Guttertown."

"I always am."

"Yeah, but you've got competition now, and he's breaking your code. Don't do anything stupid."

"You know I'm above that."

I just grunted. Neco had always been a very serious, careful kid. He'd been intense even when we were six. Now that I knew more, I was pretty sure when he pulled away and said he needed to protect his family, he was learning to sneak around and kill people. Still, Neco could be unreasonable when he wanted to be.

"You aren't any time Lance walks into a room. You're basically messy as fuck around Lance."

"That's Lance's fault."

How to say this without getting punched in the face? Ronan was the least violent of us. He got you back in different, sneaky ways. Lance and Neco went straight for the face punch. It hurt when Lance did it, but Neco was a fucking giant. He'd lay me out and it would be embarrassing because half of Guttertown was here. And I was too pretty for him to maim my face.

I stepped back and put the bar between us. Fucker had a giant arm span, but hopefully he couldn't reach me back here. And Neco loved whiskey. Maybe he wouldn't risk spilling it to hit me.

"Lance makes you messy and you make Lance messy. You

should just settle it with fists or hate fucking each other so we can all move on."

Neco looked horrified and was he blushing? I mean, I was pretty sure everyone wanted to fuck Lance. He was pretty androgynous and had both men and women flirting with him. Everyone in the tavern had asked me how to get in his pants more than once.

Problem was, if I knew that answer, I would have already gotten there myself.

"Lance is an Argent."

"Yeah."

"I'm an Argent. We could be half-brothers. A lot of shit flies in Guttertown, but not *that.*"

"Ah, fuck. That was gross. I hadn't even thought about that. Lance looks like Caitrin and you look like a giant, masculine version of Theda. I don't even think about your fathers."

"I try not to think about him, either. He never laid a hand to Momma or Rowena, but he still hurt them. He broke my code and I can't kill him. It pisses me off and I'm not nice to be around when I'm mad."

"Maybe be mad at your father and find your way towards forgiving Lance? You could be half-brothers."

Neco completely shut down. He did that sometimes. He was done. Neco drained his whiskey and stormed out of the tavern.

He wasn't any closer to forgiving Lance, but he didn't hit me and no one died, so I considered the conversation a success.

LUCY

I was able to get a ton of vodka started. I only took a break to bring Mom some dinner. She had fallen asleep in her chair fixing some holes in our clothes. The tavern was doing pretty well, but Mom had always been extra frugal. She also had money stashed all over our flat. We did what everyone did when their clothes got holes. We mended them until the whole garment was falling apart before he replaced it.

She was already in bed when I finished up in the basement and I woke up before her again. I went straight downstairs to let Athan and Tarja in. Ollie passed the message to me that they saw Theda the other day and Neco recommended some herbs. Athan and Tarja wanted to come first thing in the morning, which I thought was a little odd because I made the appointment last minute, but now I was in a panic thinking they wanted to see her first after seeing Theda.

"Relax. You look like you're about to shit yourself," Tarja said.

Tarja had the same demeanor as her brother Ilyn. I'd say that meant I preferred Athan since he was the sweetest of the siblings, but I could appreciate a woman who said what she thought, even if it was mean. I got away with it because everyone thought I was a man. I learned it from Mom and not everyone appreciated it when she did it.

There also seemed to be an age rule. Tarja was older than dirt and it seemed more acceptable to everyone when she was crass and insulting than when Mom was putting a drunk in their place. Being a woman was fucking complicated. Being me was complicated. Sometimes I felt more male than female and I definitely didn't have the equipment. Sometimes, I didn't know how I felt at all and was just existing.

"Probably because I am. My mom is coughing up blood," I shot back.

"A good reason to shit yourself, but would ruin a perfectly good pair of trousers. Let's get a look at her and maybe settle your mind," Athan said.

I didn't know how Athan was related to Tarja and Ilyn. He was also old, but had always been good natured and jovial. Athan had been better with sick kids than Tarja. Athan usually took the kids and Tarja took the adults. They were both quality healers, just with different bedside manners. I wanted both of them for Mom.

"I heard you saw Theda the other day."

"Oh, yes. But the Madame has rules at her brothel. Theda quarantined when she first got the cough, so if anyone else caught it, it was probably minor. Did you get a cough for a little while?"

"I mean, maybe? We don't have a room for sick people like the brothel, but if Mom thinks she's coming down with something, she usually tries to keep away from everyone, but especially me."

"There was something minor going around recently. Stuffy noses, body aches, and a little cough. It resolved on its own for most people, but it set an infection in Theda's lungs. It could clear up with the herbs or it could take a turn for the worse. If it gets bad, Neco will have to contact his father because of a compound she'll need. We'll have to check your mom out to know for sure it's the same with her. If it is, you're an Argent, too. You'll have to find out who your father is so you can get that compound," Athan said.

Unless I could work something out with Leodos to get the monarchy's healer to sell me this compound. Even I knew that was a longshot. Leodos was great. He didn't just look out for Guttertown. He respected my mom because he liked her spirits and he only bought them from us. He always paid her more than she asked and he taught me how to fight when I was younger.

I couldn't say the same for the monarchy. I didn't even know what they looked like. The Tempris were supposed to have red hair, but not even that would help me identify them. Rumor had it they'd been mixing with humans for so long their hair wasn't red anymore.

And a *lot* of men had a fetish of fucking a woman who could burn you to death if she lost control. It was a popular color for women to dye their hair at the brothel. The red-headed women said they made more money. There were different herbs to get red, and it was all different hues. No one knew which one was an accurate representation of Tempris red, but men didn't particularly care when it came to fantasies.

I left Athan and Tarja in our sitting room and went to wake Mom. I didn't tell her I called the healers last night because she'd get mad at me. She groaned as her eyes fluttered open.

"What is it?"

"Athan and Tarja are here to check you out."

"What'd you do that for?"

"Because you're sick. Now, get up."

"They grow up and get bossy," she grumbled, getting up and putting her robe on.

"Does anyone want tea?" I asked as she laid on the couch while they checked her out.

"I'll take a drink when we leave," Tarja said.

"You can't get drunk and see patients," Athan fussed.

"I'll do what I damned well please, old man!"

"Don't give it to her."

"Aimes said you had a new drink. I'll take payment in that," Tarja said.

"New drink?" Mom asked.

"A Bloody Mary. I've been experimenting with my new spirits. It's good."

"Aimes said it'll put hair on your chest and mess you up."

"You don't need any more hair on your chest."

Tarja thumped her brother on the head.

"You hush."

I didn't understand healers at all, so I didn't know what tests they were doing and why. It made sense to them and they had training in this. They finally stopped and told us their diagnosis.

"It's the same thing with Theda. It was the cough that was going around a few weeks ago. It morphed into an infection of the lungs. I'll tell you what herbs to get and how to make the tonic. It could clear up or it could get worse. I'll take that drink now."

I led the healers down to the tavern. I had just enough vodka to make Theda a Bloody Mary. She was peering at me while I was making her drink.

"It could get worse and it's already bad. As an Argent, you have options the rest of Guttertown doesn't. Mainly, your father. You can save your mom and lose your autonomy or she'll die if it gets bad. The compound she needs is something only the Baron's healers know how to make."

"We've been trying to come up with alternatives or how to make that compound ourselves, but we don't have the right equipment. And we can't make it without the copper. We're trying, but we're not there yet. My son has rigged something up, but we can't get our hands on the original recipe, so we're really just shooting in the dark here."

"And testing it is complicated. We need sick people to see if it would work. We'd prefer testing it on ourselves, but if we don't have the illness, it can't be us."

"I think Mom would prefer being one of your experiments to having me contact my father."

"It could cause more harm than good," Tarja said, accepting the Bloody Mary.

"Go slow with that. It's strong."

"Psh. I have a stronger constitution than Aimes. Oh, this is divine. This is going to take off."

Ollie came in because it was time for him to get started. He grinned when he saw Tarja and Athan because he knew why they were here.

"Who is that stunning woman enjoying our new beverage?"

"I'm not drunk enough to believe a strapping young man thinks I'm stunning. You don't need to flirt. The drink speaks for itself."

I started laughing. Did I just meet a woman who was immune to Ollie? He shot me a filthy look because he knew why I was laughing.

"Fuck you, Lance," he muttered.

"I'm going to talk to Mom. We made a pact to never take away the other's choice when I was ten. I kind of did that calling the two of you, but I don't regret it. She's *never* wanted me to have to contact my father. I think she'd be willing to try the remedies you're cooking up, and she'd prefer it over my going to my father."

I couldn't lose her. She took my choice away when she raised me as a boy and never told me until she couldn't keep that secret from me anymore. Mom promised to never do that to me again, and I swore I'd do the same with her.

She played an extremely risky game when I was younger,

but it was a lot harder to keep a secret now that I'd gone through puberty. It would be nearly impossible if I got conscripted into my father's army, but I could do it.

Mom was up and making something to eat when I got back upstairs.

"No more healers unless they are from Guttertown. I don't want you contacting your father, Lucy. I mean it. I wasn't with him because I wanted to be. He wasn't some charming, handsome man that swooped into Guttertown and I fell in love, but was smart enough to keep an exit plan when he left.

"I know that's the big story with Guttertown women and the Argent kids. That we fall for their sexual prowess and lies because we're stupid. That's not how it goes *at all.* The Barons come here and fixate on a woman. We *can't* say no or they will make our lives miserable. Theda didn't fall for it twice. She didn't have a choice the first time or the second.

"Ever wonder why the brothels don't have babies running around all over the place and women who don't want babies never end up with them except for when the Barons are involved? The royal family has only been able to have one child. They aren't not having sex after they have the one.

"The herbs to stop a baby are very effective if used correctly. I can't prove this, but the Barons profit off their illegitimate children *every* time. I'm pretty sure they are messing with those herbs the women are taking because Theda and I have always been friends, and we were taking ours faithfully. That's the kind of man you're dealing with. I don't want you going to him."

"I don't *want* to go to him but I don't want to lose you, either. Athan and Tarja are working on some experimental remedies, but they said the Barons have a compound that could cure you. Tarja and Athan said what they are working on could cure you or kill you. They can't test it on themselves because they aren't sick. You'd be their test subject.

I'm not taking your choice away, but I am giving you options."

"We both know if I do nothing, you're going to go straight to your father, my one and only. I know you're bull-headed and do what you think is best because you got that from me. I don't want to die, either. Your father is dangerous. He's the worst of all the Barons and you're a woman, sweetie. He's only going to have one use for you if he finds out. Athan and Tarja are brilliant. They are really only limited by their equipment. If it comes down to it, I want their remedies, no matter how experimental, over all the strings that would come with the one your father would give."

I had to tell her. I told her everything.

"I asked Leodos if he could get something from the royal healer."

"Leodos is a good man, and he speaks highly of the princess and king, but that's not going to happen. The royal healer might work for the palace and treat the monarchy, but we don't know what the stock of him is. The Barons want the Tempris off the throne. They've probably got the healer in their pocket, reporting any sickness and how close they are to losing their magic.

"They'd report back that they were asked to make a compound when the royal family wasn't sick. They'd probably get a pretty penny for it, too. With the Princess Lisana missing, they'd cause a stink and they could use it to say Joron and Esylle have been keeping her hidden. At the least, they'd look into who it was for and when they traced it back to you, they'd make you pay it back, even if you already paid the healer."

"Fuck. I hate Nestran sometimes. We outnumber the Barons. I don't see why we don't just rise up and get rid of them."

"Dangerous talk, Lucy. It sounds easy, but it's not. You'd have to find someone everyone in Nestran could rally behind. I'm talking *all* of Nestran. You'd have to unite the merchants, artisans, farmers, Guttertown, *and* the shifters to work together. We all hate them, but those groups all hate each other, too. Some of those groups would hate someone who tried to unite all of them simply because of where they're from or what magic they have. The person you're looking for doesn't exist."

"One day, things are going to get bad enough that they do."

"Well, when that day happens, you can convince Guttertown to join their cause."

"You can join me because I refuse to lose you."

I did. Plan A with Leodos was a bust. I got why it wouldn't work. Plan B was Athan and Tarja.

Hopefully, I never had to move to plan C, which was betraying Mom and losing my freedom.

BECK

Half of Guttertown couldn't stop talking about some weird new beverage Lance cooked up that sounded a lot like drinking alcoholic soup. Lance had a head for business. Ollie would be the soul of the Whispering Raven who flirted with everyone and made it a pleasant place to eat and get drunk, but Lance was the brains and that had everything to do with Caitrin.

I was planning on swinging by because I was just as worried about Caitrin as I was about Theda. Our mothers had all been friends, and that was how we ended up a group when we were younger. My mom helped raise my friends just as much as Caitrin, Theda, Ollie's parents and then aunt and uncle, and Ronan's parents raised me.

Theda wasn't doing that great. Mom wouldn't let her work. Athan said she wasn't contagious, but the cough could get worse and kill her. Mom took care of her girls, so she wasn't going to kick Theda out or force Rowena to do anything. She'd been paying Neco as a bodyguard as long as she'd been paying me.

I checked in on Theda and tried to comfort Neco and Rowena. Neco tried to pull me aside.

"Ollie has a big mouth," Neco growled.

"That's not new."

"I *know* you know."

Ah, fuck. I really didn't want to deal with a cornered killer who seemed to be really good at it.

"I don't care. In fact, the next time they are in here hurting our girls, I wouldn't mind tagging along."

Neco just smirked at me and he had no right to be that sexy.

"You'll have to ask your Aunt Keeva to train you so you'll be good at it."

What.

The.

Fuck.

Aunt Keeva was a marshmallow who always had sweets for me. She was one of the kindest people I knew. When I was little, I found a bird with its wing hurt and I bought it straight to her because I thought she was the best person to fix it. She did.

"Don't talk about Aunt Keeva like that."

"I asked Panas to train me to be an assassin when he was teaching me to fight. He sent me straight to Keeva. Panas said the people of the Jagged Key Isles had certain skills when they came to Nestran. Your family was a mix of warriors, assassins, and business people. They passed those skills down through the generations just in case."

"I liked you better when I thought you were just a serial killer. I can't believe you just told me that my favorite aunt trained you."

"Your aunt is fierce, and she also makes a mean cookie."

"I hate you."

"No, you don't."

"You're right, I don't. Anyway, none of us are going to betray you."

"Lance might if he finds out."

I didn't think Lance and Neco actually hated each other. Lance wouldn't turn him in if he knew. They were both pig-headed and had hurt each other. Neither were willing to apologize because they thought they had been wronged worse.

If Neco wasn't a serial killer and Lance wouldn't cut me off at the Whispering Raven, I'd thump them both in the head and tie them up in the basement until they worked their shit out. But like, thoroughly tie them down because I knew about my Jagged Key Isles ancestors and if Keeva taught Neco to be an assassin, she's probably taught him how to slip bindings.

I was having a serious talk with my aunt tomorrow.

"Lance won't. How's Theda?"

"Too early to tell if the herbs are working or not. My father is a total shit, but I have no problem asking him for the compound if needed. I just have to negotiate *me* paying it back and him never coming for Rowena. If she ever works for your mom, it's going to be because *she* wants to, but right now, she's got an apprenticeship lined up with Ollie's uncle with his horses."

"Well, half the men who come in here to pay for sex are terrified of her. The horses wouldn't stand a chance."

They were. For a ten-year-old, she was pretty formidable.

"I know, right?" Neco said, puffing up his chest.

"I'm going to check on Caitrin."

"Let me know how she is? I might hate Lance, but Caitrin was always good to me."

Liar. Lance and Neco told anyone who *didn't* ask how much they hated each other. I'm pretty sure there was something more going on there, but Neco and Lance were both impossible to read most of the time.

"Will do. And I know you love to talk about how much

you hate Lance, but he's gifted with spirits and recipes. He's got some new weird drink that has Aimes's seal of approval."

"That doesn't count. He'd drink piss if it got him drunk."

"No, he wouldn't. You're still mad he pulled you aside and tore you a new arsehole after you broke Lance's nose."

Neco just grunted.

"Why does *everyone* side with Lance about that?" he grumbled.

"You had every right to break his nose. He was a shit for what he said. You're *both* dicks for letting this feud go on this long. Ronan has been helping out in the tavern and Lance has mostly been in the basement making spirits. You could come with me. It's Tuesday, so it's going to be slow and mostly Guttertown regulars. Panas can handle it."

"Deal, but if Lance is there, I'm leaving."

It was a start. Some of the girls in the brothel were in relationships. I had no idea why I could fix it when someone's boyfriend had done something really idiotic, but I couldn't mend the relationship between my oldest friends.

We walked next door to the tavern, and I was shocked when we got through the front door. The tavern was usually busy around this time, but it was outright packed tonight. There were bodies smashed everywhere together drinking what looked like blood and everyone was pretty drunk. Ronan was running around like a chicken with its head cut off and Ollie looked overwhelmed at the bar.

We had to squeeze into the bar, but everyone knew who we were. They parted for us and gave us a space. I wasn't even sure most of these people knew Neco was murdering people in the Trulos District, but they knew not to mess with either of us. Neco because he was giant and intense and me because I was of Jagged Key Isles blood. They knew we were fierce fighters.

And apparently, my Aunt Keeva could bake an amazing cake and slit a man's throat without leaving any evidence. I was still reeling from that. I shouldn't be shocked because I knew my people had that knowledge, I just didn't think it was Aunt Keeva who knew that shit.

"Guys, you know how Lance gets crazy ideas sometimes? I thought he was insane, but the new drink tastes amazing and it'll fuck you up fast. He's working on a sweet version, but the recipe isn't to his liking yet. Ronan and I got here early and mashed tomatoes for hours. If you want a Bloody Mary, get on it now because we're almost out and I'm not mashing more tomatoes."

"I'll take one."

"Me, too," Neco said.

Because Neco might talk about how much he hated Lance, even when no one asked him, but even Neco could admit Lance had magic when it came to spirits. It wasn't the same kind of magic the Tempris or the shifters had, but it was still magic.

"Coming right up!"

Ronan flew up to the bar looking harried.

"Are we out? Everyone is drunk and in love with Bloody Marys. They may start eating people if we don't have anymore. I don't want to get eaten, Ollie!"

"Beck and Neco got the last of it."

"Good! Everyone is scared of Beck and Neco. If they get the last of it, they can protect us when we tell everyone we're out."

Ronan hated fighting and avoided it when he could. I got it. He made his living with his hands and made beautiful things. Ronan didn't hit people like the rest of us. He played the long game and got people back later.

"We'll do it," I said.

"Same. I owe you for Rowena's party."

None of us would ever be able to afford Ronan's art. Not the way he deserved to be paid for it. We could make damned sure he could continue to make it, though. Ollie slid the beverages over.

"Take it slow. Lance cooked up something more potent than Caitrin's whiskey."

Trust Lance to try to do that. Leodos grew up with everything Baron life had to offer and he currently lived in the palace. He swore by Caitrin's whiskey and wouldn't drink anything else. He said the quality was better than anything in Nestran and the people he shared his flask with agreed with him until they found out he bought it in Guttertown.

I was looking at the Bloody Mary suspiciously, but Neco had always been a little unhinged. Ollie warned him, but he just upended the tankard and gulped it down. He slammed the tankard down and his whole body shuddered.

"So, Lance is still a shit and I hate him, but that is *potent* and tastes amazing!" Neco yelled, hooting.

Fuck me. We had a drunk serial killer in a crowded bar. I took a sip of mine because I really didn't want one of these drunk people to start shit with me over what was the last Bloody Mary and at least one of us needed to be sober.

It *shouldn't* taste good, but it did. You could barely taste the alcohol, but you could certainly feel it. Lance was a genius, but I wasn't here to get drunk. Lance would also break my nose if I disturbed him while he was working in the basement to ask about Caitrin. Ollie would know. He knew everyone's business.

"It's the same thing Theda has. Athan and Tarja are working on something, but it's experimental and could do more harm than good. They'd prefer testing it on themselves, but they don't have the same sickness. It's messy. Caitrin can either risk it and take the experimental remedy or Lance can contact his father for a cure everyone knows works. I get the feeling Caitrin told him who his father is, and he's particularly bad as far as Barons go."

"Who is Lance's father?" Neco demanded.

We'd seen the man who kept coming around Neco's when we were kids. We knew he was a Baron because of his clothes, but Neco refused to tell us his name before he pulled away. He was only ever in Guttertown for Theda and no one spoke to the Barons if they deemed us worthy of their presence unless they spoke to us first. We only got their names if they gave it to us.

I knew what Neco's father looked like, but I still didn't know his name. Ollie didn't, either. And Ollie also didn't know who Lance's father was. Which was weird because Ollie tended to know everyone's secrets.

"No idea, man. He hasn't said. Just like you haven't."

"Is Lance going to hit me if I go down there?"

"Wait until closing," Ollie said. "He's been working himself to the bone with this new spirit and he hasn't been in a good mood. We'll go down there with you. If you promise to behave, you can come with us, Neco."

"Nope," Neco slurred. "I don't want to damage that pretty face breaking his nose again."

Neco was drunk as fuck and seemed really annoyed Lance was so good looking. Yeah, I knew the feeling. We *all* wanted to kiss Lance, but we didn't want to ruin our friendship.

I wondered if Lance felt the same way about Neco's face and they might eventually hate fuck their way back to each other.

LUCY

I was bone tired and frustrated as fuck. I'd made an arrangement with Athan and Tarja. I was doing *all* of this with the spirits to save Mom because I thought I could pay a healer without going to my father. That was out, but instead of moving immediately to Plan C and violating Mom's trust, I skipped it and went to Plan D.

That was the plan where I used the extra money we were making to help fund Athan and Tarja's research. It was what Mom would have wanted. I could hear what was going on above me in the tavern. The Bloody Mary was doing great. The Whispering Raven was packed.

I wrapped things up and was about to go up and help Ollie and Ronan clean when Ollie, Ronan, and Beck came down to me. I was happy to see them and I *knew* that, but I was also in a terrible fucking mood. I was crampy, so I knew my period was about to start anyway. Mom taught me how to track it so I'd know, but mine had always had a mind of its own.

Even my mom couldn't figure out how to predict when this evil would arrive. Sometimes, it would skip a month and when it did show up, it wasn't with enough regularity for anyone to guess when. Mom and I could usually figure it out because I was a raging arsehole and my lower back would hurt. The cramps had started, too, so it would probably be within the next few days so I could prepare.

"Hey, I was about to come up and help you clean."

"I'll do that," Beck said. "How's Caitrin?"

I couldn't just sit there and bawl my eyes out with my friends. I was definitely feeling more female than male right now. How stupid was it that guys couldn't cry when they needed to and be comforted by their guy friends? Because I needed that right now.

"I've been busting my ass trying to make money with the tavern for a cure. That's what the Bloody Marys and the recipe I'm tweaking is for. I know Athan and Tarja don't have access to the same equipment the rest of Nestran does. I'm doing all of this to avoid asking my father. Mom doesn't want me to. She's all but forbade me.

"My father would be the only one with a sure thing to cure her, but he wouldn't take the money I'm making, even if it was enough to cover it. He would profit off me more if he refused to give me a sum and kept me working until I ended up like Aimes.

"So, I'm doing *all* of this to help Athan and Tarja work out something and hope they get it right and that in the process, their experiments don't kill her first. I'm a mess and I'm just trying to keep it together because I'm all Mom's got. I can't lose her."

"Hey," Beck said, squeezing my shoulder. "Caitrin gave birth to you, but she's practically our mom too. I'm helping with Theda because she's my mom, too. Let us help."

"Listen, first of all, fuck Neco Argent, but I love his mom. Don't tell him, but I'm doing this for Theda, too."

Yeah, fuck Neco, but I was doing this for him, too. Neco had always been a momma's boy, but not in a weird way. It was always more of this intense kid who recognized his father fucked over his mother and stepped up to protect her, though he couldn't even protect himself.

When I'd sneak into his room at night, he'd tell me all about how he was going to be rich one day and take care of his mom so she never had to work or worry again. All that was shattered when his father showed back up in their lives and ruined everything.

I might hate him, but it would *destroy* Neco to lose Theda and no Argent kid wanted another to have to deal with their father. It was the principle of the thing.

"Go upstairs and take care of Caitrin. We'll clean the tavern. We're going to have to make a better plan for the Bloody Marys because making the tomato juice takes time. Ronan and I made a ton while we were waiting for everyone to get off work and come and we still ran out in three hours. I'll also have to talk to my uncle about the tomato and potato supply to keep it going."

"Thanks, guys. Give me a night to catch up on sleep. I've got a lot of barrels made and my infusions just need time before I can test them. I'll be more help tomorrow."

I really needed a hug from my friends, but I had these stupid tits. They were smashed to my chest with bandages that had left me with permanent scars, but still. I couldn't get a proper hug from anyone but Mom.

I got up to leave and for some reason, Ollie jumped up and practically pressed himself to my back. It seemed like he was going to follow me home.

"What are you doing?" I asked.

"Just trust me. Get upstairs immediately."

Ollie had some pretty stupid ideas sometimes that ended up with us spending a night in the cells, but he *always* looked out for his friends. This wasn't silly Ollie. This was protective Ollie, so I just did what he asked.

He was so close to my back on the stairs that we were both

in danger of falling, but when I got to the door, he shoved me through it and slammed it behind me. It was weird, but I was exhausted and I'd find out what that was all about in the morning.

When I got upstairs and went to change into my sleeping clothes, I figured it out. My stupid period had come when I was working. I'd bled through my trousers and Ollie saw.

And since he didn't rag me about shitting my pants and tried to protect me, one of my best friends had just figured out I was a girl.

OLIVER

Holy shit. It *all* made sense. Why everyone wanted Lance and Lance didn't take them up on it. Why everyone wanted *me* except for Lance. Lance wasn't Lance. Lance had been a girl this entire time.

Mind

Blown.

The Madame kept all the sex stuff away from us when we were kids, but she made damned sure all us boys weren't grossed out by a woman's bodily functions and knew periods were perfectly natural. I'd gone with Beck to pick up supplies for the girls plenty of times.

I knew exactly what I was seeing on the back of Lance's pants, but I also knew if he wanted us to know that, he would have told us. Fuck, did I call Lance 'he' or 'she?' What did Lance prefer? I didn't know why we spent our entire lives thinking Lance was male.

I also knew Lance was going to need some things, so I lied to Beck and asked to buy some herbs for a tea that would help and just told him it was for a girl I was secretly seeing. The Madame also made sure we'd be able to care for our future wives when they were going through this instead of fucking off to the tavern or brothel like some of her customers. Beck's mom would have Panas beat our asses if we got married and showed up to her brothel while our women were hurting.

The Madame was probably more terrifying than Panas, so we all listened when she taught us.

I went back to the tavern and braced myself to go talk to Lance. Lance would have figured out I knew by now. Lance was probably flipping out, and I needed them to know I wasn't going to tell anyone. I was dying to know, but they didn't need to tell me why. All they needed to know was that their secret was safe with me.

I brought the tea and my best puppy dog face when I knocked. Lance might really be a girl, but if they wanted to punch me in the face, I already knew it hurt because they'd done it plenty of times. When Lance opened the door a crack, I could tell they'd been crying. Yeah, fuck that.

I muscled my way inside, set the tea on the table, and crushed them in a hug. Did Lance never hug us like we hugged each other because they were worried we would find out his secret? Lance collapsed in my arms, sobbing. I just held them up and squeezed them.

"Hey, it's not a big deal. You don't have to tell me why if you don't want. You just need to tell me if you want me to call you a girl or a boy. Your secret is safe with me."

I guided Lance over to the sofa and sat them down. I didn't let them sit alone. I'd been in love with Lance for years, but right now, they needed a friend. I wrapped my arm around Lance and pulled them to my chest.

"My real name is Lucy, but you can't call me that unless we're alone."

"Pretty name. Are you okay, Lucy? I know you didn't mean for me to find out this way. I brought tea the girls at the brothels use to help with their periods."

"I didn't start out lying to you. I didn't *know* I wasn't a boy until Mom couldn't keep it a secret anymore."

That didn't sound like Caitrin. Caitrin was a strong momma bear and she would have loved her child even if they were a girl. If the Tempris heir was a girl, she took the throne with her husband as a consort, but the Barons didn't let their female children inherit anything. They married them off for power and money. It wasn't like that in Guttertown. I couldn't think of any reason Caitrin would do that to her child.

Lucy saw how I was looking at her.

"She thought she was protecting me from my father. She has the same story as Theda and countless other Guttertown women. The Barons come here when their wives are with child and set their sights on a woman. She couldn't exactly say no and had to pretend to like him and lay underneath him when he wanted it. They *always* end up pregnant and Mom thinks it's because they are messing with their herbs.

"The Barons *keep* doing this in Guttertown because they know we're poor and we'll eventually need their help. They can work us until we can't just because they can. Mom isn't stupid. She knew it may eventually come to me asking him. If he thinks I'm a boy, he'll put me in his army or maybe somewhere a smaller man would make him money.

"As a woman? He'd whore me out in the brothels. I'd have no choice and the Madame couldn't refuse it. Mom said if I ended up working there, it was going to be because I wanted to and the only money I'd be losing was the part that went to the Madame because she takes care of her girls. She'd be damned if I worked there because I was forced and my father was profiting off of it."

That was more like the Caitrin I grew up around. The fierce momma bear who did crazy shit to protect her kid. All of our parents were like that, even mine before they died.

Tricking Lucy into thinking they were a boy was pretty wild, though.

"What Caitrin did was completely insane, but I guess I get why she did it."

"You know why I hate Neco so much?"

Maybe if I found that out, I could fix this thing with Lucy and Neco. I managed to patch things up with Neco and Ronan.

"I was feeling really weird and achy when Neco cut us off. We used to sneak into each other's bedroom at night. He locked the window and ignored me that night. The next day at school, my body and my mind were hurting. I didn't *mean* to lash out at Neco, but I did.

"He broke my nose instead of letting me apologize. I went to Ilyn for something for the pain and I didn't know how he was about blood. Ilyn chewed me out and kicked me out of his shop. I found out I wasn't a boy that night because my period started and I thought I was dying. Mom explained she'd lied to me for my entire life and why. I associate *all* of that with Neco breaking my nose."

Fuck. I could have Neco groveling at Lucy's feet in five seconds by informing him he'd broken a girl's nose, but I wouldn't do that to Lucy.

"Do you prefer being Lance or Lucy?"

"I only get to be Lucy around Mom. Most of the time, I'm pretending to be a man. I don't tell her this because she feels bad about taking my choice away and lying to me, but it's actually confusing as fuck. I don't actually know because I don't get to be Lucy...ever unless I'm at home."

"You can be Lucy around me. Beck and Ronan would keep your secret, too. They'd be happy to let you explore if you'd rather be Lucy or Lance."

"For what it's worth, Mom has *always* wanted me to tell all of you."

"Why didn't you? We wouldn't have given a shit and we

would have helped. We've *all* been in love with Lance for years. You know we're all together, right? We wanted Lance to be a part of that, but we didn't want to ruin the friendship."

"What the fuck, Ollie? You've got a big fucking mouth, and I didn't know you were all together? Your big fucking mouth is one of the reasons I didn't tell you."

Yeah, I was offended. I heard a lot of gossip at the bar. Sometimes, I heard things I couldn't unhear. I really didn't want to know about Lovel and Earline's sexual escapades because the visuals were *haunting,* but if they wasted perfectly good lard and got creative with the soup ladle, they gave me all the graphic details.

"First of all, I only repeat the things I hear to my closest friends because I know you're not going to spread it around. Secondly, you know Ronan lives for that shit. Thirdly, I never talk about *our* business. We knew pretty much everyone in Guttertown was interested in Lance, but Lance didn't seem interested in anyone. We didn't want you to feel left out because we were all together, but we always wanted you to join."

Lucy started laughing.

"You put *Lance* in a horrifically awkward position when you all decided to lose your virginity at the brothel. I never got with anyone because they couldn't see me naked."

Since Lucy was spilling secrets, this was a juicy one I *had* to know.

"Well, *Lance* is a fucking legend at the brothel because that girl told everyone what happened. Since I know the Lucy secret, I need to know that one because I'll bet it's juicy."

"I'm guessing you know how to pleasure Beck and Ronan because you're a man and they are men. I just did to her what I'd want to be done to me and then gave her a massage to avoid getting naked."

Being a twenty-year-old man sucked sometimes. I was trying to comfort the person I'd been in love with for years and they were talking about girl-on-girl action. My brain knew I should change the subject and not make a big deal about it, but my cock wanted Lucy to describe it to me in graphic detail.

So, I just laughed instead.

"We talked behind your back for weeks. It was a disaster for the rest of us. I barely lasted two seconds, and she still looked bored. It was the same for Ronan. Beck knew he was terrible, but she faked it because of his mom. That fucked Beck up for a while."

"Can I tell you another big secret since I seem to be in a sharing mood and you managed to find out I'm not Lance?"

"Well, I told you several of mine. It's not as big as you not being Lance, but you could destroy me with it."

Oh, splendid mother of fuck. Lucy snaked into my lap and straddled me. I'd wanted this for *years* and I was still terrified of ruining it.

"I've been secretly in love with all of you, too. Mom knew. She can see right through me. It's why she always pestered me to confess. You know, I kissed a woman that night at the brothel, but that was the one time I've ever kissed anyone and I've never kissed a man before. I'm curious."

Oh, shit. Of all the times I dreamed about this, I never thought Lance would be Lucy or that it would actually happen. I needed to make it a good once since this was her first kiss with a man. Thankfully, I wasn't the same sixteen-year-old who managed to bore a sex worker in three thrusts.

I grabbed her and yanked her down to me. I devoured her mouth. She must have tested one of her infusions before she came up because she tasted like mangoes, apples, and mint. Lance was mostly hands off if anyone hit on him, but Lucy was responsive as fuck. She ground on my cock and I was willing to take this as far as she wanted to go.

I groaned when she pulled away.

"Sorry. As you saw, I'm on my period."

"That doesn't bother me."

"Uh, it bothers me. I don't want my first time having sex to be while I'm on my period. My periods are *terrible.*"

"Then you need to finish that tea. I'll pick up more from Ilyn so you have more while you're working tomorrow. You don't have to worry about me spilling your secret. I've been calling you Lance for so long, it shouldn't be a problem to keep doing it in public until you ask me to stop."

"Ollie? When we're alone, call me Lucy. No one calls me Lucy except for Mom. Sometimes, it feels like I'm lost in being Lance and I don't know who I am."

"Anything you want. I'm never going to pressure you. But if you let Ronan and Beck in on your secret, you'd have more people who could help you figure out if you want to be Lucy or Lance."

Because I wanted to help. I loved Lance and Lance was Lucy. Beck and Ronan would love her either way. Lucy needed us. I got what Caitrin was trying to do pretending Lucy was Lance. I didn't have to ask because I knew Caitrin would have given her child the choice once she knew the truth. Lucy decided to keep the ruse up, but it sounded like it was messing her up and she wasn't talking about it with Caitrin.

"I know. Just give me time. I'm dealing with so much shit. Can we do this again?" she asked, nuzzling my chest.

"Any time you want."

It was such a mess. I kept a lot of secrets but I didn't usually keep secrets from my friends. I was lying to Lucy about Neco and I was lying to everyone else about Lucy.

I really couldn't fuck this up or they'd both be in danger.

LUCY

Ollie had been nothing short of perfect after he found out my secret. He brought me tea that helped and was completely supportive. Ollie also pointed out he didn't blab to *everyone* just us. And apparently, I was going to have to eat crow. My friends were in love with me, too. Mom had been right the entire time.

Which meant I was going to have to get up the courage to tell the rest of my friends. The herbs must have been helping Mom because she was awake and had breakfast made. I fussed at her anyway.

"You should be resting."

"You need to spill the details about Ollie's late-night visit, my only child."

"How did you—?"

"I'm your mother. I know everything."

"Ugh. Ollie figured out I'm a girl."

"How did he do that?"

"My stupid fucking idiotic period. I want a refund that I have to deal with that. We should be able to cancel that contract if we want to."

"You have been a little more snippy than usual. Did it sneak up on you?"

"Yeah. After Ollie left, I had to scrub blood out of my pants."

"Sorry your cycle is so difficult, my love."

I took a deep break. This was a big step for me.

"I'm thinking of inviting Ollie, Beck, and Ronan for dinner and answering the door as Lucy."

"Well, out of all your friends, Ollie was going to be the most dramatic about you not being a man and it sounded like he handled it beautifully."

I sighed. He really did. And I hadn't forgotten what it was like to kiss him. Yet another reason it was fucking stupid for my period to be an unbreakable contract for the next twenty to thirty years. If I was really Lance, I wouldn't have to deal with it.

"Ollie was great. And he's not going to tell anyone. He said his big mouth is only for us. He tells *us* everyone's business because Ronan always wants to know, but he never tells anyone else. I'd be safe telling them."

"I've always known that, but I also know something else."

"What's that?"

"You'd be *happy* telling them. Lucy is beautiful, and she deserves to be seen. It sounded like the tavern was packed last night. I can help tonight."

No, she couldn't. She had a little more color in her cheeks and she didn't sleep in, but as soon as she said that, she had another coughing fit and she couldn't hide the blood this time with me this close. It wasn't gushing out of her mouth and was just a little, but it still terrified me.

"Absolutely not. Not until you stop coughing blood. I've got enough vodka made to last us for a little while and my infusions aren't perfect yet. *I* will be the one helping in the tavern."

"On your period? You'll start a tavern fight and spend a night in the cells. At most, you'll break my tavern."

"Oh, shut up. I'm not that bad."

"Jorah Pickerin still doesn't know why you snapped and broke his face when you were twelve, but I do."

"That wasn't because of my period. Jorah was making fun of Neco and his mom. I might hate Neco, but no one should be allowed to say those things about anyone. Theda isn't stupid and Neco isn't weak."

"That's my girl."

"I have to go help Ollie and Ronan. Making the mixture for the Bloody Marys takes a lot of time. They premade a bunch beforehand, and we still sold out in three hours. Ollie's pretty face and silver tongue managed to prevent a riot, but they will all be back tonight and they might bring friends."

"I'm proud of you."

I puffed up my chest and hugged her. That was all I ever wanted. For my mom to be proud of me. Ronan was surrounded by tomatoes when I went downstairs and I couldn't find Ollie, so I asked.

"So, Ollie got really good at fixing farm equipment and rigging things up to get things done faster. He brought a wagon of garbage from the farm because he thinks he can rig something up to deal with all these fucking tomatoes."

"Seriously? That would be amazing."

"I know. If my back hurts, I prefer it to be because I was making something beautiful, not making tomato juice. You just didn't *see* the garbage he brought in. I had to talk him out of putting it in your basement because if he broke something, the tavern would be out of money and you'd kill him. He's in the kitchen."

"Hey, can you come for dinner tomorrow? It's the Day of Respect, so we have to close early. I was going to invite Beck and Ollie, too."

The Day of Respect was such shit. It happened every

Saturday. No one was allowed to work after two in the afternoon. The rest of the day, we were supposed to give thanks and respect to the Barons who protected us. Not the king or queen, the Barons.

I heard Guttertown used to ignore that because some people couldn't afford that, but they sent guards here for the Day or Respect to enforce it. They had for as long as I'd been alive. I guess the guard didn't get the day off.

Ronan just scoffed.

"I know Caitrin is too sick to cook, but none of us are fucking stupid. We aren't going to say no to a home-cooked meal from you, either. Listen, I'm not trying to be demanding, but can you do that mango custard your mom used to make when we were kids?"

Ronan was looking at me with puppy dog eyes. He'd always had a sweet tooth, and it wasn't hard to make at all.

"Sure. Any other requests?"

"I've been itching for a swim. If I catch them, will you make lemon and fennel clams?"

"Uh, yeah. Especially since I wouldn't have to pay for them."

"You're the best, Lance. If Ollie gets his garbage working, then I can get my swim in."

Ronan was part fish. We used to go swimming all the time when I didn't know I should be embarrassed to be topless around my friends. Then, I grew tits. The whole thing was stupid. If I could be topless as Lance, why was it unacceptable for me to be topless as Lucy? People missed the whole point of boobs.

"Go swim, Ronan. It's how you center yourself. I have faith Ollie will get a machine up and it's not going to get really busy here until people get off of work."

Ronan beamed at me. He was also insanely good looking. Ollie was a fair golden boy with tanned skin and Beck was dark with his hair to his waist. Ronan was about as close to being a redhead as a human could be without being Tempris. Humans didn't have red hair, but Ronan was close and it was always in his face. He also had bright-green eyes. It seems like every time he went for a swim, he came back with more freckles.

I went to the kitchen to check on Ollie. Unlike Ronan, I'd personally seen Ollie unleash his creativity on farm garbage and rig up something that benefitted their farm and this tavern. I leaned against the door and just watched him work.

"I'm going to tell Ronan and Beck tomorrow. You're invited to dinner. I'm cooking. I sent Ronan to swim because he was getting antsy."

"No shit? For what it's worth, I'm glad. They'll keep your secret and help you figure out if you want to be Lucy or Lance. I speak for all of us when I say we don't care which one you pick."

"Thanks. We've got another hour before any of the early birds come in. I'm going to walk next door and invited Beck. I'll lock the door behind me."

"Good. If you see Neco, *please* just ignore him."

Ugh. I wished my mortal enemy didn't live in the same building as one of my best friends who I had been secretly in love with for years. It would make it *so* much easier to pretend like Neco Argent didn't exist and ignore the fact that he had this really annoying dark, broody sexy thing going on. It made me hate him even more.

When I got to the brothel, Rowena was leaving for school.

"Hey, Rowena."

That fucking kid. She punched me right in the tit. My eyes watered and I tried not to let on why it hurt more than it should.

"*That* is for being mean to my brother. I didn't kick you in the dick because you brought Mom soup. Consider yourself lucky," she said, glaring at me before stomping off.

Even though she just assaulted my left boob, I still liked that kid. She was plucky. Honestly, she thought she was doing me a favor not kicking me in the dick, but since I didn't have one, I would have preferred it over the tit punch.

When I turned around, Neco was leaning against the wall smirking at me.

"First of all, fuck you," I said. "Secondly, bye."

I stormed off to find Beck. I could hear Neco laughing at my back all the way down the hall. I found the Madame before I found Beck.

"Goodness, you look like you're in a mood, Lance."

"Neco Argent has that effect on me."

"Really? Everyone here loves him. You have to be careful the kind of men you let work here. They are here all the time and they protect the girls. Some of the girls get attached. I don't forbid that, but a lesser man would use the opportunity to take advantage of my girls for free sex.

"Panas isn't interested in woman sexually. Beck knows I would kill him if he did that. I gave Neco a chance because I knew him as a boy. It could have gone completely wrong and I might have had to throw him out, but the man he grew into is the same ten-year-old boy who lost an eye trying to protect his mom. He's nothing but respectful and I don't think he's ever laid a finger on one of my girls, even if they asked him to. And many of them are very interested in him."

"There's no accounting for taste."

The Madame just laughed.

"Neco Argent has those dark dangerous vibes that say he would burn the whole realm down for the right person. It has its appeal. If I was a *much* younger woman and didn't help change that boy's diapers..."

You shouldn't be shocked by anything out of Beck's mom's mouth, but somehow, you always were. Even when she was protecting us from all the inappropriate things in her business, she still managed to scandalize the kids without even mentioning sex. I honestly thought it was one of her kinks. She just threw back her head and laughed because I was standing there with my mouth open trying to process that.

"Beck is in the kitchen eating breakfast. I'm guessing you're here for him, though I think Asha would be thrilled if you were back for her..."

"Going to find Beck now."

The longer I stood here, the worse the Madame was going to get. I seriously thought she did this because she was trying to see if she could literally make a man's head explode. I wasn't even a man, but that was definitely me who went down on Myrna and it was weird hearing your best friend's mom sexualizing your mortal enemy.

I knew where the kitchen was. I ate there with my friends plenty of times. Beck was eating eggs and bacon and looked surprised when I joined him.

"I thought you'd be preparing for your new hit drink."

"Ollie brought garbage."

"And you let him inside with it?"

"He's super talented with scraps. You remember how we all used to beg your mom to make that Jagged Key Isles crab recipe, and she got tired of us asking, so she said she'd only make it if we brought her the crabs?"

"Oh, shit! Yeah, none of us had jobs to buy them. We told Ollie our moms would beat our asses if he stole them so he rigged up that crab trap from scraps at the farm."

"He's actually really good at that. He could actually make a fair bit of coin selling his inventions, but he prefers the tavern. I have full faith he's going to build something that makes it easy to make the Bloody Marys."

"Sorry, Lance, you know I love you, but I've known you my entire life. You're a bit of a control freak. You wouldn't be over here talking to me and leaving Ollie alone in the tavern with garbage unless something was up."

"I'm cooking dinner on the Day of Respect and you're all invited. Ollie and Ronan are both coming and Ronan has already put in his requests. If you say no, I'll rope your mom into convincing you."

"That's low, Lance. Everyone is terrified of Mom. And I'm not stupid. If you or your mom wants to cook for me, you don't need to blackmail me. Just say when."

I gave him the time and went back to check on Ollie. The Day of Respect was idiotic because all the businesses had to close and no one could work. The brothel and the tavern made most of our money hours after we were all forced to close and pay respect to the Barons. It was like losing an entire day of income once a week.

But it was the one night a week Ollie, Beck, and I could hang out because we weren't working until late. It was the one silver lining to an utterly shit situation.

Ollie really was a genius. In the time I was at the brothel getting tit punched, scandalized by the Madame, and inviting Beck to dinner, Ollie already had something put together that made making the mixture *much* easier and could make much more of it than we could by hand. He'd already made a good bit of it.

"Good, you're back. You put the tomatoes, here and then you turn this crank. It'll press them through the mesh into the bucket and then you can just dump it in a barrel."

I took a chance because Ollie really was a good kisser and I wasn't going to get the chance to kiss many people who knew the truth about me. And I just really loved Ollie.

I wrapped my arms around his waist.

"You really are a genius. You could probably make a lot of money selling those inventions. More than you make slinging drinks at the tavern."

"But then I couldn't be around one of my favorite people when they aren't in the basement and making these things make my back hurt. It's not as fun as slinging drinks. This tavern is my parents' legacy. Your mom made sure I got to keep it after they passed and I'm not going to throw that away for something that doesn't make me completely happy."

"Well, you look sexy surrounded by garbage *and* slinging drinks. Kiss me."

Ollie was a great kisser. He was passionate, but he took his time and didn't rush. I wanted more. I was probably the only twenty-year-old virgin in Guttertown. We tended to get that out of the way early here. We didn't keep to the same purity nonsense for women that the rest of Nestran subscribed to. I mean, I was only holding onto it because I didn't want anyone to know I wasn't a man.

And fucking Ollie stopped me when I went for the laces on his trousers.

"Your first time having sex isn't going to be in the kitchen of a tavern."

I shoved Ollie away because that was just *so fucking stupid*. I wasn't even going to have sex because I was still on my period. I just wanted to see what sucking cock was like.

"You had absolutely no problem with Lance losing his virginity at the brothel. Why are you holding Lucy to a different standard?"

"Because we shouldn't have roped Lance into it. We all had our regrets about it. We turned it into this big rite of passage thing that was going to change our lives and we pressured you into it. We thought it was different for you because you got turned into this legend, but we were just annoying teenagers to those girls.

"One of many clients that night. We knew they were faking it and we were terrible. It felt good, but it also felt terrible because those women knew what good sex was and we didn't give it to them. I don't want that for your first time. I want us to *both* feel good and I can't do that in a kitchen."

"That makes sense. How good are you going to make it feel?"

"You know how Lance is a legend at the brothel because of

one little visit when he was sixteen? We all learned how to take care of women like that later."

"When do you think that is going to happen?" I asked, sliding back into Ollie's arms.

"In my uncle's barn after dinner. It's going to have to be with all of us. They'd beat my ass if it was just me."

"You seem pretty sure they are going to accept Lucy."

"You should be, too. They are going to love Lucy."

I wished I was as sure as Ollie was.

BECK

onan was bouncing around my bedroom as we got
ready for dinner. Usually, it was Ollie doing that.
Ronan was convinced something was up for
dinner. We usually hung out on the Day of Respect, but
Lance never went full out and cooked a meal for us. Ollie
should have been the one running around with conspiracy
theories about why Lance was being so nice.

Which could only mean one thing.

"You know something."

"I know a lot of things."

"You'd better spill," Ronan said, tackling Ollie.

Because if Ollie was being obtuse, he was keeping secrets.
Ollie just laughed and wrestled with Ronan. Then he pulled a
low blow and went straight for a crotch massage to calm
Ronan down. Ronan moaned.

"That's not fair."

"We need to leave. Seriously, just be patient."

I grabbed the tin of Walnut and Honey buns my mom made. My friends really liked them and Mom said it would be rude to show up empty-handed. We walked next door and walked upstairs to Lance's flat.

I was utterly gobsmacked when Lance opened the door wearing a dress. At first, I thought Lance was trying to tell us that he liked wearing women's clothing, which wasn't a big deal in Guttertown, but Lance had a pretty luscious pair of tits on him.

Ronan and I just stood there with our mouths open. Lance was a pretty man, but they were gorgeous as a woman. Was this even Lance? Did Lance have a sister? I'd known Lance my entire life. I'd know if they were a woman. Ollie swooped in and kissed the woman on the cheek.

"Hi, Lucy. We should get inside because it's not safe. Someone could see her."

I was still processing, but I stepped inside with Ronan. I knew every plane of Lance's face because I'd been in love with them for years. Unless Lance had a hidden twin, this was Lance. And Lance wasn't here. Ollie called them Lucy.

"Hi," Lucy said.

Yeah, Lucy was Lance. Or Lance was Lucy. I knew that voice. It was musical and she must have deepened it a little when she was Lance, but this was definitely my best friend and the person I'd been in love with.

"Uh, why are you a girl?" Ronan asked. "Not that I'm complaining because you're stunning and it changes nothing."

"Come eat and I'll explain."

Lucy explained over a pretty elaborate dinner—by Guttertown standards—why we all thought she was Lance and why it still needed to stay a secret. Caitrin wasn't with us. She showed up long enough to take a plate to her bedroom.

Lucy was brutally honest, and I got it. Mom would have wanted to protect her and she wouldn't have been able to. Lucy's father would have squeezed the brothel until she had to close. It would have pissed off every man in Nestran, but they would have played it like it was her fault the brothel closed and not that she refused to let one of them exploit their daughter.

It sucked, but Mom had to think about *all* of her girls. She'd fiercely protect any one of them, but not at the expense of all of them. Some of her girls worked there because they wanted to and some because they didn't have any other options. If someone wasn't completely sure about working at her brothel, she'd try to give them other options first.

The Baron's daughters were a totally different beast. Mom's hands were tied. She couldn't tell the Barons no and she couldn't give them another option if they didn't want to do it. Mom hated it and so did everyone who worked at the brothel.

"I get it better than the others," I said. "Those girls with other life plans that have their choice taken from them never end up lasting very long. They fade into nothing until they are a shell of themselves. Mom and the previous Madames have gone to bat for them with their fathers and tried to tell them they were going to end up dead. The Barons don't care and those girls all die way too soon."

The rest of Nestran thought it was shameful to work in the brothel, but it wasn't in Guttertown. It was good money and a roof over your head paid for by the men who thought it was shameful. But it wasn't for everyone and it needed to be *her* choice. It sounded like Caitrin made sure if Lucy ever made that choice, it would be hers.

But Lucy wasn't done yet. She had more to tell us. She hadn't just been pretending when we were kids. Lucy legitimately thought she was a boy. We always thought it was weird Lance didn't just whip it out to take a piss when we were playing and always went somewhere to do it alone, but we thought he was just shy.

Caitrin told Lucy that was private. She should do it away from us and leave if we were doing it to keep her secret, so she didn't know she was different. And then Ronan and I officially found out why Lance was so volatile around Neco. It was a lot to unpack. And Neco would probably grovel to the ends of the realm if he found out Lance was Lucy because his whole thing was killing men who hurt women.

But that would involve betraying Lucy's trust and telling us this was pretty major considering what was at stake.

"Ollie found out by accident, but I'm telling the rest of you for a reason. The first reason is because I love you and the second is because I'm Lance all the time. I can only be Lucy at home. It's confusing. I feel like I'm two people and two genders and I don't know who I'm supposed to be. I need to be Lucy more, even if I can't do that in public."

"We can do that," Ronan said.

"Definitely," Ollie said.

I agreed, and I got where she was confused. It would probably fuck my head up to be one gender to the public and another in private. But I had a feeling who Lucy was where it counted was exactly who Lance was. I was guessing Lucy was just as pig-headed and calculating as Lance.

And it didn't matter if she was Lucy or Lance. It was the brain inside that head that had all the brilliant ideas for the tavern. All the things that made my friend an intelligent, kind person had nothing to do with them being a man or woman. I'd happily help Lucy wade through the complexities of her dual identity but I was pretty sure there was more overlap there than she was giving herself credit for.

"That's not the best part," Ollie said with a shit-eating grin on his face.

Lucy turned purple, and it was pretty hard to make Lance blush. I mean, I grew up in a brothel and we played there often as kids. There was also Guttertown in general and the fact that some pretty wild shit went down at the tavern she lived in. It was hard to make *any* of us blush. Lucy blushing was about as unsettling as Neco Argent blushing, just for different reasons.

"I told her we were all in love with Lance," Ollie announced.

Fuck. Could I get Neco to break his rules and kill Ollie? Having Neco in my bed sometimes recently was already a perk, but I should really be able to ask him to kill my other boyfriend when he ran his big fat mouth to someone I wanted to be in a relationship with. And I wasn't stupid. I knew how fucked up *all* of that was.

"Relax. Lucy *and* Lance feel the same. Lance was just stand offish with us because of Lucy."

"It sounds so fucked up when you say it like that," Lucy moaned into her hands.

"It's really not because I promised Lucy a special night in my barn and we've always done *everything* together. Lance has always been able to handle us no matter what we got up to. Can Lucy?"

"You want me to lose my virginity to *all* of you?"

I wasn't mad at that idea. We all regretted how *we* did it. We got Mom's permission, but that didn't change the fact that to all the women who worked there, I was the Madame's kid and the rest of them were boys they watched play as kids.

At sixteen, we were all so excited to have sex for the first time, we weren't thinking about how weird we were making it for the women. Even at twenty-years-old and a trained warrior, they'd probably think it was weird if I wanted to pay for a night with them. Neco and Lucy as Lance seemed to be the exceptions. We could do it right for Lucy.

"I mean, it goes without saying I'm your favorite," Ollie said. "You just can't say that out loud. I don't want to fight Beck if it was just me and fucking Ronan would find a way to get me in the cells for a week as payback. And we'd never ask you to pick."

"The person who never backed down from anything has always been *you*," Ronan said.

"Is that crazy?" Lucy asked.

"No," I said. "We all love each other, it's just some of us are finally admitting it. We'd never ask you to pick. And I know exactly how we're going to play this if you agree."

This played out better than I could have hoped. And Ollie made sure if she wanted to explore being Lucy sexually for the first time, we were all there. We'd all get our moments with Lucy alone, but for the first time, it should be all of us.

I guess I could save asking Neco to kill Ollie the next time one of his stupid ideas landed us in the cells again.

LUCY

We didn't have story books in Guttertown, so we loved our gossip. That was why I changed out of my dress and back into trousers and a shirt before we walked to the barn. I knew damned well the gossip mongers weren't going to immediately jump to the truth, but Lance had a reputation for being a pretty boy and some people had a fetish for that. It got weird sometimes.

They wouldn't immediately jump to Lance being Lucy, but they *would* start some stories about Lance liking to wear women's clothing. Which people did in Guttertown and there was nothing wrong with it, but it was a little too close to the truth for me.

We were laughing and joking as we walked to the farm. It was nice. It felt like a weight had been lifted off my shoulders. It wasn't that I hated Lance. I just never got a chance to be Lucy.

A giant blur came running at me and tackled me. I landed on my back with a thud and I could hear three men growling behind me. I punched the person on top of me. They just laughed and hauled me to my feet.

"Hey, little brother."

"Autar? I gave you one black eye. Who gave you the other?"

"So, I'm the general now. It sucks, but I meet all kinds of pretty women. I asked one to marry me and she hit me. She had a hell of a right hook. I think I'm in love."

"Hold up. What the fuck? Autar is your brother?" Ronan asked.

"Half-brother," we both said.

We knew they wouldn't ask us for our father's name. No one ever said it out loud if they could avoid it. Autar only told me the first time because I was also an Argent kid and he was pretty drunk.

"Oh, that's delicious," Ollie said. "You look nothing alike. Autar is a mountain."

"Yeah, but Lance shares my affinity with the ladies. He's a legend at the brothel," Autar said, punching me in the arm.

"Your black eye says otherwise," Beck pointed out.

"She was just flirting. It's foreplay."

"I don't think so," I said.

"That's because despite being a legend at the brothel, you really don't understand women. Anyway, I have to get back to my post. How stupid is the Day of Respect? Bye, brother!"

"Is he for real?" Ronan asked. "He just tackled you!"

"Nothing you haven't done before and I gave him a black eye."

"Yeah, but Autar is a fucking giant."

"And he thinks you don't understand women," Ollie giggled.

"Yeah, yeah," I said, jumping on Ollie's back and putting him in a headlock.

Ollie wrapped his arms around my thighs and took off running towards the farm.

"Nothing is keeping me from this. Not even your massive brother."

Ronan and Beck were running beside us hooting.

"You'd better put me down or you're going to be too tired to perform."

I wasn't a small person. Yeah, I was thin, but I was also muscular and tall.

"Psh. I'd never be too tired for that."

Ollie finally set me down when the farm was in sight. We went straight to the barn. I was expecting the usual barn, but Ollie had gone all out. He'd made a mattress out of hay and covered it with blankets. Ollie had lanterns hanging from hooks in the rafters. He walked over to a table with bottles on it and lit a small candle underneath an oil burner.

The Madame had these at the brothel. It was a Jagged Key Isles thing that some people in Guttertown had adopted if they weren't as dirt poor as everyone else. It made the entire house smell wonderful. The Jagged Key Isles people sold oil that smelled like rich spices from their home, but you could also buy some that made it smell like you had been baking.

I preferred the rich spices from the Jagged Key Isles and had made no secret about it. I bought the kind that smelled like baking for the tavern because it was welcoming and sometimes, people came straight from work without washing. The oil covered up most of the body odor. Ollie got the kind I preferred, and it filled the barn.

Fuck me. I was nervous. I mean, it *should* go down like this. We'd been inseparable since we were toddlers and I'd never want to choose between them. They were all very different men. I loved them for different reasons. They could all destroy me the same.

At my infamous night at the brothel when we were sixteen, yeah, I went down on her, but we also just talked while I rubbed her back. I knew the first time hurt. She also said there were ways it could hurt after the first time, too.

I trusted them and I was fine with a little pain. Problem was, I wasn't sure what would happen to that trust if it were a lot of pain. I knew everything about them except all the intimate stuff that was never a possibility until they knew my secret.

Beck stepped forward and kissed me. Beck kissed differently than Ollie, but he was very good at it. That just left Ronan, but Beck was blocking his way.

"I have an idea, but it's up to you. It'll take a lot of trust from you."

"I'm open to hearing it, but I may say no."

"Okay, so there are definitely ways for the three of us to share you that we'll get to later, but are probably a little much considering you haven't done this before. There's probably going to be plenty of times it's just you with one of us, but this needs to be all of us.

"We are *never* going to ask you to pick. So, my suggestion is that we blindfold you. You won't know who is touching you or which order we go in. I promise you, every one of us knows how to make you feel good and we've shared women before. We would have invited Lance, but we didn't think he'd be into it and if we knew about Lucy, we never would have touched those other women."

"And trust me when I say we're motivated to make this the best for you," Ollie said. "We've been in love with you for years when we thought you were Lance. We want to do this a *lot* with you and we're never going to look at another woman again."

"Some women like being blindfolded even when they are just with one man," Ronan said.

I thought about it. Someone would have to go first and I certainly didn't want to pick. I trusted these guys. I also knew Beck's entire job was stepping in if things went too far. He wouldn't let things get painful for me. I didn't *think* they would, but I'd also had a conversation at the brothel when I was alone with one of the girls. She said sometimes, men had an entirely different side to them when they got naked.

"Let's do it."

Beck ripped his shirt off and tore the bottom off. I gasped because it was a nice shirt and you just didn't intentionally fuck your clothes up in Guttertown. The brothel and the tavern were probably the most profitable businesses, but we still mended the holes in our clothes until they completely fell apart. We weren't royalty or the Barons. I heard some of those women had dresses they only wore once. What a waste.

Beck just smirked at me.

"Was the gasp because I look good without my shirt on or because I improvised because I don't have a blindfold."

"I got so distracted you ripped a perfectly good shirt just to blindfold me during sex, I didn't have time to check you out. And I've seen you without your shirt plenty of times. You know damned well you look good."

Ollie ripped his shirt off next and gave me his perfect, pouty face.

"Check me out and tell me I'm pretty next."

"I'll only tell you that you're pretty because you're sulking. All of Guttertown is in agreement on that and tell you all the time."

"Yeah, but it doesn't count when drunk old Dot Barclay tells me I'm pretty and pinches my arse. It only matters when *you* do it."

"And me," Ronan said, spanking Ollie's bottom. "I'm secure and don't need you to stroke my ego, but I won't complain if you do."

"And I won't complain if all of you get naked so I can properly look," I said.

Oh, wow. They were apparently just as excited as I was because they were already stripping before I could even finish my sentence. They were naked before I knew it. I guess it was my turn. I went for my shirt, but they stopped me.

"Oh, no. We want to undress you."

I had to bind my chest again when I changed clothes. I

might be thin and muscular, but I had tits that couldn't be hidden with a baggy shirt unless they were strapped down. They noticed when they peeled my shirt off.

"Is this necessary?" Beck asked. "I could ask the girls about some kind of corset."

"We already tried that. They amplify cleavage and shove them up. Corsets make them more noticeable. I need them strapped down."

"It looks uncomfortable," Ronan said.

"It is, but I'm used to it."

"Let us get you out of that," Ollie said.

It was always an enormous relief when the bindings came off, but this was different. Ollie was tender when he unwrapped the bandages. I only had them on long enough to walk to the farm, but they'd already caused redness and indentations on my skin. He noticed the scars.

"Lucy," he whispered, caressing my ribs. "I hate that you have to endure this."

"It's better when they are off."

"Then when you are at any of our places, they are off," Ronan said.

"Everyone knows better than to go into a room without knocking at the brothel. And honestly, I think everyone there would get why you're Lance outside your flat, so they'd keep your secret if they ever found out."

I was trying to resist the urge to cover myself with my arms. I'd been strapping my breasts down and been seriously annoyed with them for so long, it was just weird standing here topless. Ollie caught my arms when they moved to cover me.

"Don't do that. This is natural. This is you. You're beautiful and you don't have to hide from us."

Ronan came up behind me and started kissing my neck.

"You really are perfect. Don't hide from us."

Beck started pulling at the laces of my trousers.

"Let us see you. May I?"

I nodded, but then Ronan started nibbling on my shoulder. I really loved that. Ronan held me up as I leaned back into him and Beck and Ollie pulled my trousers off.

"Ready for that blindfold?" Beck asked.

"I mean, yeah. You destroyed your shirt for it."

Beck passed the blindfold to Ronan, who tied it around my eyes. Ollie scooped me up and carried me to his blankets. He set me down gently and they all pounced. There were mouths and hands all over me.

Someone was kissing me, another person was sucking my nipples, and another was between my legs nipping at my thighs. It was almost too much. I let out a huge moan when whoever was between my legs started flicking my clit with their tongue.

Whoever was kissing me had my hands pinned down. I could have figured it out by touching their hair. Beck's was in locs down to his waist, Ollie wore his tied back in a strip, and Ronan kept his short. They knew that and they were keeping my hands out of the equation.

I had been a little unsure of the blindfold, but I actually loved it. I had no idea when or where the next touch was coming. Someone was licking my clit and had a death grip on my thighs, but the other two? I didn't know what they were going to do next.

They were flicking my nipples with their tongues or biting my neck. I'd never done this before, so I didn't know what I liked. I was figuring it out and so were they. They were learning every single cry and moan I made.

Someone slid a finger inside me. I felt a small pinch, but it wasn't terrible. I grew up riding horses on Ollie's farm and fighting with an evil donkey. There probably wouldn't be much in the way of blood. He let me adjust and then added another finger. It felt fucking amazing.

I knew what an orgasm was because I'd experimented in

bed and I played in a brothel as a kid, but the one that hit me curled my toes and arched my back.

"Fuck!" I yelled.

"Don't wake my uncle or he'll see your tits," Ollie said.

Ollie was the one holding my arms down and kissing my neck.

"Shut up!" Ronan hissed.

Ronan had been the one worshipping my breasts. That left Beck with the talented tongue between my legs. They pulled away so we could all regroup.

"Are you ready for us?"

I started giggling.

"You can't disguise your voice from me, Ollie, but yes, I'm ready."

I couldn't tell if it was Ollie or Ronan first. I'd always know Beck because of the baths he took in perfumed oils. It didn't matter. The person who went first was gentle with me, but it was also passionate. He took his time, and I appreciated it.

I was guessing Ronan, but I didn't know for sure. Someone had my hands pinned down so I couldn't touch him and figure it out. And I was still learning what I liked, but I was very much into being blindfolded and helpless right now. Mostly because I wasn't really helpless. If I wanted my hands back or the blindfold off, I just had to ask.

The man who went first was perfect. He left my body singing and shaking. They were pretty firm on keeping their identity hidden from me. He panted, but I could tell he was trying to keep any noises he made to himself so I couldn't guess. I still didn't know if it was Ollie or Ronan.

When the next man came to me, I instantly knew it was Beck, and I didn't have to touch him or hear him. I wasn't sure if he knew about this ahead of time if he would have skipped the scented bath that gave him away. Beck always smelled like sandalwood, cashmeran, and spices. That scent always smelled like home, but I'd never tell them that was how I identified Beck.

Beck apparently, had different ideas. He wouldn't speak because he still didn't realize I knew it was him. I couldn't see what he was doing, either. He gently picked me up. I went along with it, even though I didn't know what he was about to do.

Beck placed me so that I was straddling his waist. I got it. He wanted me on top. That fateful night in the brothel when I ate out one of the girls and gave her a massage, she told me that was the favorite position of most of the girls there, but they didn't get asked to do it very often.

I couldn't see, so Ollie and Ronan guided Beck inside me and helped me get situated. It was awkward at first, but it was pretty easy to figure out what to do. And fuck me. I could see why all the women at the brothel liked this position. It felt fantastic and was perfect if you happened to be a bit of a control freak...which I was.

I threw back my head and just enjoyed the ride. I was having the time of my life. Maybe there was one good thing about my cursed period. It exposed me to Ollie and led me to telling my friends the truth. It led me to this barn.

Beck was growling and gripping my hips. I could tell he was trying not to make any noise because they were committed to me not knowing who was who. He wanted to me to go faster, but he'd never tell me that with this blindfold on, so he just manipulated my hips how he wanted it.

I was so close. I almost forgot there were two other men in here, but in this position, they had ample access to my body. I had a mouth on each nipple and it pushed me over the edge. The barn was pretty far away from the main house, so hopefully, Ollie's uncle didn't hear me crying out. I couldn't exactly keep it in.

I draped myself across Beck's chest and tried to catch my breath. His scented skin smelled even better when it smelled like sex. But they weren't done with me and they didn't give me time to rest for very long.

I might be blindfolded, but I knew these men. The hands that picked me up and set me down on all fours were calloused. That meant it was Ronan who went first and Ollie who was touching me now. Ronan had elegant, artist hands. Ollie spent his life on the farm after his parents died. He worked at the tavern now, but he worked with his hands a lot, rigging things up for the tavern and helping out at the farm when he could.

I had an idea the first man was Ronan because of how passionate and gentle he was. Ronan was always like that unless you wronged him. He never got angry or lost his cool. He just got even without throwing a single punch like the rest of us.

Ronan was passionate like an artist and Ollie was more like a fire. It made sense that Ollie would go last. I guess they wanted me to experience a variety of positions tonight or share their favorites with me. Ollie wanted to take me from behind. Beck and Ronan didn't want him to do that alone.

One of them was kissing me and the other was pinching my nipples as Ollie slid into me. All three positions felt differ- ent. Ollie was hitting something inside me that felt good, but he didn't stop there. He finally spoke and confirmed I was right. He tried to disguise his voice, but he'd never been able to hide from me.

"Get her clit."

Someone leaned forward and started massaging my clit while Ollie pounded into me. He was a little rougher than Ronan, but not out of control. I liked it. I heard him snarl and yelped when his hand came down to spank me. Except I actu- ally liked it.

"Do that again," I panted.

I wore my hair short. Some guys in Nestran wore it long, but my face was a little too feminine to pull it off while pretending to be a boy. The person in front of me tangled their hands in my hair and pulled. Ooh. I liked that, too. They kissed me passionately.

I exploded again. I honestly didn't think I could cum again. This was what? The fourth time tonight? My body was shaking through the aftershocks. They pulled the blindfold off and immediately snuggled me.

"Did we do good?" Ronan asked.

"It was perfect. We're definitely going to have to do that again."

"First things first," Ollie said, handing me his flask. "Drink this. I made the tea you'll need not to get pregnant."

"Thanks."

Because honestly, I hadn't even thought about that. Having sex had been off the table for so long, I hadn't really worried about getting pregnant. My period showed up with a vengeance, but it never lasted long. Since it was impossible to track, Mom told me if I ever started having sex, to make sure I had the tea.

"I wouldn't be mad if you had my baby," Beck said, tracing my stomach with his finger.

"I'm not ready for everyone to find out I'm Lucy, but I'm glad all of you did."

I really was. I was a few steps closer to figuring out who I was.

RONAN

I didn't peg Lance for Lucy, but I really liked Lucy. She was basically still my best friend who I'd been in love with forever, I just had to touch her differently and I was perfectly okay with that. She basically spoke and acted like the same person I grew up with.

We slept in Ollie's uncle's barn. We did that a lot after Ollie moved in with his uncle, but it was very different this time. The Day of Respect was officially over, so Guttertown had to work extra to make up for all the tasks they didn't finish or all the income we lost when we were supposed to be paying our reverence to a bunch of people we wouldn't piss on if they were on fire.

It was a hot mess. But I had a line on a job that was probably going to be a lot of fun. Beck told me to come to the brothel after we woke up because his mom was interested in hiring me. She was probably one of the few people in Guttertown who could afford art.

The Madame was a classy lady. She never went anywhere without looking impeccable. She'd never cut her hair and wore it in locs like all the Jagged Key Isles people in Guttertown. The Madame took the same perfumed baths that Beck did. It was always great for the Guttertown economy when she wanted a little redesign on the brothel.

Ollie's aunt just assumed we were recreating our childhood sleepovers in their barn. She fed us and sent us off to work this time instead of school. We walked back into town together. Ollie and Lucy split off to the tavern and Beck and I walked into the brothel.

Yeah, the Madame was definitely redecorating. There were bolts of fabric leaning against the wall and she looked happier than usual to see me. I think *all* of us adored her as kids and grew up to admire her.

"Ronan, dear, come sit and talk."

On my way to join the Madame on the couch, Neco was coming out with Rowena to send her to school. A well-dressed man who definitely wasn't from Guttertown mowed right into Rowena and sent her flying on her arse. He was completely at fault and to me, it looked like he had done it on purpose. But he didn't stop there.

"Gutter brat," he said, spitting on Rowena. "You're going to end up a filthy whore like everyone here."

Rowena wasn't the kind of kid that would cry because some rich merchant spat on her and insulted her. She was madder than a wet cat and if Neco hadn't escorting him out while he was shrieking about how he was a paying customer, Rowena *would* have assaulted him. This was the type of man who would want severe punishment for a child that fought back after he deliberately knocked her down and insulted her.

He was also dumb as fuck because he did it in front of Neco. Neco would escort him out in a way that he couldn't press charges and then sneak into his house in the dead of night and slit his throat. This was a dead man walking, and I wasn't mad about it.

Maybe it said something about me that I didn't follow them out and try to warn this man that a giant with one eye had marked him for death, but I honestly didn't give a shit. Rowena had picked up that Neco ignored me in public and automatically assumed I'd done something horrible to her big brother.

When she was all of five, she marched straight up to me and punched me right in the dick for hurting her brother. Rowena assaulted Ollie once, too. It wouldn't shock me if she hit Lucy because Lucy and Neco fought like cats and dogs. Beck was probably the only person in our group she actually liked and that was only because she could see that Neco liked him.

Even a five-year-old's dick punch hurt like fuck, but I still liked that kid. She had spunk. If she'd hit that merchant after he knocked her down and Neco wasn't around, I would have tried to take care of it myself and probably hanged for it.

I sat across from the Madame, but my gaze was still on Rowena. She looked like she was trying to find another dick to punch, so I crossed my legs just in case she didn't know Neco and me had made our peace.

"That man doesn't realize what kind of demon he just awoke," the Madame said, clucking her tongue.

That was when it hit me. She knew what Neco's extracurricular activities were. We should have realized that. If Beck figured it out, his mom probably figured it out much sooner. That woman seemed to have eyes and ears everywhere. Sometimes, she knew about Ollie's shenanigans before he could rope us into them.

Of *course,* she knew Neco was murdering her clients. She just didn't particularly care to say anything to him about it because the Madame didn't want that kind of business. I couldn't say I blamed her.

"He's not going to know or realize it until it's too late," I said.

There was only a tiny bit of surprise on the Madame's face before she hid it. I was surprised I even got that. The Madame didn't fight with her fists. She was a master of wits. I wasn't about to play that game with her, so I directed the conversation away from Neco and the fact that he liked to murder people and back to what she needed from me.

"So, I'm tired of the wallpaper. It makes me angry just looking at it and I loved it two years ago. The fables of the Jagged Key Isles aren't like Nestran. There are no damsels being rescued from monsters by brave men. They are a lot racier than Guttertown stories, so sometimes, the damsel ends up happily married to the monster who treats her like a queen.

"It's all a metaphor for who the actual monsters are, of course, just like all fables and fairy tales are meant to teach a lesson. My ancestors left the Jagged Key Isles because their government was just as bad as the Barons here. It was the same thing. The Barons have the shifters painted as the monsters and the Jagged Key Isles did that to my people, so we left.

"The Jagged Key Isles fables are fun, but they would also be shocking to everyone in Nestran except for Guttertown. I've decided I want to replace the wallpaper I can't stand with murals of those fables. I'll pay you well."

Oh, my fuck, I *adored* Beck's mom.

"You're seriously going to *pay* me to paint murals on the wall of damsels getting railed by dragons? That's the second greatest thing to happen to me this week."

"What's the first?"

Finding out Lance was Lucy, she returned our feelings, and our night in the barn, but I'd never say that. Though, it wouldn't totally shock me if the Madame already knew that. She knew more secrets than Ollie.

"I can't reveal that under threat of death."

Seriously, Lance might be Lucy, but she was pretty good at

outright brawling. If she wanted revenge, she could beat my arse in a fight easily.

"Then keep that secret close to you. Yes, I want to pay you for that. It's a lot of fables and I want them all over the brothel. This would be a long-term job. You let me know what supplies you'd need and I'll get them. I'm used to feeding you, so the kitchen is open to you when you need it. I'm also not going to complain if you want to take a break and unwind at the tavern. I've been meaning to walk over myself to try Lance's new drink."

"That's *way* more than generous."

"No, it's not. You aren't the only Guttertown artist. The rest of them are making clothes, perfumes, and metal work. You're the only stubborn individual who decided they were going to make something just for the beauty of looking at it.

"There are only a few people who can leave Guttertown and do business with the rest of Nestran. Most of them are the Baron's children they had in Guttertown and I'm one of the other ones. You managed to do it on your own. We're proud of you. This will get your work out to people outside of Nestran who treat this place like their dirty little secret."

"Oh, wow. Thank you."

Seriously. She was getting a lot of art from me, but I was also getting months of work, free food, and a *lot* of exposure. Sometimes, people tried to cheap out on paying me by saying people would see my art on their walls and *they* would want to hire me. But if everyone paid me in just exposure, I'd starve to death.

"You earned it and I'm getting plenty out of it. Get me a list and I'll send Beck for the supplies. I've hired someone to come in to pull the old wallpaper down and prepare the walls for you. You should be able to get started soon."

"I'll need to know all the fables you want. I'm pretty sure you didn't tell us the monster-fucking stories when we were kids."

"No, I definitely didn't. I'm sending you to my sister. She's a better storyteller than me and she has cookies. Take Beck. He's had a lot of questions about his aunt lately that she needs to answer."

Keeva was everyone's favorite aunt. She ran an amazing bakery, and she always had a sweet for us when we were little. Ollie might hear all the secrets, but I adored being up in everyone's business and hearing them. I wasn't going to do anything with that information, but it wasn't like I could walk to a book shop and buy something. I loved drama when it didn't involve me.

I wanted to hear Keeva tell me stories again, and I wanted to know what kinds of questions Beck had about her.

Overall, this had been the best two days of my life.

LUCY

I was deliciously sore, but in a good way. As soon as we got home, I went upstairs to check on Mom. She was still sleeping, and she looked paler than when I left last night. I trusted Athan and Tarja, but their herbs weren't helping. At most, they were treating the symptoms, but not the infection, I needed to check with them on their new remedies. Tarja usually came in to drink when she got off, so I could ask then.

We'd be losing Ronan at the tavern. The Madame had always been supportive of Ronan's art, but she wouldn't have asked Ronan to come in for a job unless it was art related. If Ronan had asked her instead of Ollie and me, she would have put him to work, but she would have known we'd always let him work at the tavern if he needed it. The Madame wouldn't have stolen him from the tavern unless she had a good reason.

Ollie and I were prepping for the day. I had stew starting and bread baking while he used his contraption to squeeze tomatoes. It was nice. I walked over and kissed his cheek because there was one thing I needed to do.

"I need to check my infusions. I'll be right back."

"I demand to taste it if it's delicious."

I smacked his butt on the way out.

"You know you're my official taste tester. I'll be back up."

I pulled my infusions out to strain them. I officially had the infusion time down. Just mango was good, but it wasn't what I was looking for. The other wasn't it, either. The mango, apple, and mint was the closest, but it still wasn't perfect. It would probably be just right if I threw a cardamom and nutmeg pod in with everything.

I had a *lot* of supplies in the basement, so I got a new batch started and went back upstairs to help Ollie. Ronan had joined us and I hadn't seen him this excited in a long time. He filled me in on what the Madame had hired him to do and I was just so happy for him.

Ronan loved that kind of art and I knew the Madame would pay well. I was still getting used to them knowing the truth about me. Ronan was so excited, he scooped me up and spun me around. When he set me down, he gave me a passionate kiss.

"Hey, don't leave me out," Ollie sulked.

"Then, get over here and make your move."

Ollie jumped up and smashed me between him and Ronan. Ronan was kissing my mouth and Ollie was kissing my neck. Ronan groaned and pulled away.

"Beck and I have to go see Keeva so she can tell me the fables I'll be painting. Apparently, Beck has some questions for his aunt. Later, okay?"

"I know everyone says it's painful to turn men on and leave them hanging, but it's not really fair for women, either," I moaned.

"Do you have a fetish for kitchen sex? This is the *second* time you've tried to get me naked in the kitchen," Ollie said.

I punched him in the stomach.

"I'd avoid pissing me off and getting naked somewhere I have easy access to a meat cleaver."

"You're bluffing. *No one* who has experienced my dick

wants to cut it off because they'd miss it. And anyone who sees it for the first time is thinking nice thoughts, not cock-chopping thoughts."

"Ollie thinks his dick changes lives," Ronan snickered.

"It does! But you know sometimes my temper gets the best of me. I want to experience it again, so don't poke me."

"Um, Lucy, the whole point of my cock is to poke you with it. It's kind of how that works."

"I'm going to actually kill you."

"No, you won't."

"Lance could kick our asses, so Lucy can, too. She might not cut your dick off, but she can beat you in a fight."

"True," Ollie said. "It was hot when it was Lance, but it's sexy as fuck knowing it was really Lucy. Wanna wrestle?"

"Wanna wrestle all the angry drunk people if we can't make enough Bloody Marys again?"

"Eww. Why did you have to put that visual in my head when I was trying to be sexy?"

"Would you rather the visual or would you rather be full-body tackled by Leland Strain after he's come straight from mucking out the pig stalls and has had a few in him?"

Ollie shuddered.

"You're just mean today."

"She's not wrong, either," Ronan said. "Leland gets mean when he's drunk."

"You're both wrong for bringing that up when I was trying to get Lucy naked."

"We need rules," I said. "We're together, but we're also running a business. I need the business to be successful because Mom is sick and I never want to have to contact my father. My mom never wanted it and I don't, either. When we're supposed to be working, we're *working*. Outside of work, we can get up to the other stuff."

"I can agree with that, but I'm still going to flirt."

"Me, too, and probably some kissing, but nothing that takes away from our tasks."

"That's an excellent solution," Ronan said. "I have to go. Beck was in the bathtub when I left, but he should be out now. You take care of your work and I need to handle mine."

I was alone with Ollie again. His contraption really was amazing for making what we needed for the Bloody Marys in mass quantities. I just hoped we didn't run out again. If I could get my infusion recipe just right, I knew it would be just as much of a hit and bring enough money to get Athan and Tarja whatever they needed to cure Mom.

I just needed to get the recipe right first and then make mass quantities of it.

NECO

I t felt *good* to have a new target again. Momma was still sick, and I was getting closer to having to suck it up and ask my father for help. I didn't have much to offer him to keep Rowena out of it permanently. He'd want me in his army because of my size. I was good at killing and shit at following orders. I couldn't exactly brag about my skill set as an assassin because I was just a Guttertown bastard and expendable. I'd hang, and he'd take his payment from Rowena.

And Lance Fucking Argent was everywhere lately. I could usually avoid him and he kept popping up like a bedroom disease. Everyone was raving about the Whispering Raven's new drink. It sounded pretty weird, but it was delicious. I couldn't even get my whiskey because Lance crawled out of his basement to help out in the tavern.

I was on edge and really needed to kill someone.

Daegal Highmore came to the brothel early and fell right into my lap like a present. Panas might have been the one to catch him and kick him out instead of me. Beck was taking his bath, and I was going to walk Rowena to school. It was usually slow first thing in the morning.

But no, that prim fucker decided he was going to go after *my* little sister. What an idiot. If he would have hurt one of the adults, Panas would have eventually told me and we still would have ended up here, but he touched my sister and *spat* on her right in front of me.

Rowena punched me in the stomach and put several curses on me on the way to school because I didn't let her punch him in the dick, but my baby sister didn't need to know I'd be slitting his throat later. She looked up to me enough that when I told her it would be handled, she trusted me and stopped putting it out there that my nuts should grow pustules and fall off.

When she was older and could handle it, we'd get a good laugh about how I slit his throat for laying his hands on her.

They didn't give names at the brothel and if they did, they were fake. That didn't stop me. Keeva taught me well. I knew who he was, what he did, and how to get into his house before I went back to the brothel for lunch.

I also gathered a little intel on my competition. I'd eventually kill him, too. I wouldn't usually care if someone else was killing rich prats outside of Guttertown. They were awful. I wasn't stupid. Their wives were probably awful and their kids were probably snotty little shits.

Their wives and kids didn't have the power to be as big a shit as the men. That's just how things were outside of Guttertown. You didn't hurt women and kids. They would probably spit on me, too, if they heard me speaking with a Guttertown accent, but if those men were hurting women in Guttertown, they were probably doing it at home, also. They needed my protection as well.

Daegal was the typical rich merchant, but he was on the richer side. He puffed up his chest and liked to pretend he was just as important as the Barons, but he was licking their boots just like the rest of the Trulos District. The Barons weren't going to pay him just like they weren't going to pay anyone else. They were probably taxing him within an inch of his life and lying to his face that he was getting a better rate.

He was definitely the dumbass for believing it.

I went home with a sense of satisfaction. I wasn't all that sold on the nickname they gave me, but people were afraid of the demon sneaking into their house and slitting their throats without leaving any evidence.

It was this other man who was killing in my territory who was pissing me off. It was wrecking *everything*. I killed for a reason. Men in the Trulos District could do what they wanted to women because they were considered their property, but there was always the risk of a father or brother taking offense. In Guttertown, there were no consequences.

If this interloper wasn't murdering on my territory, *someone* might figure out why the Blight was slitting throats. They'd never catch me. Keeva made damned sure of that. But if they knew why the Blight was killing people, they might stop being utter shitheads.

It was genius. Don't hit people who didn't deserve it because you needed to feel like a big man and the demon wouldn't slit your throat. It was a *big* motivator. Maybe I should write a manifesto.

I probably should. I managed to catch gossip on my way out of the Trulos District. They thought we were the same person which was just fucking insulting. That other guy was *messy* and he would eventually be caught. Whether it was by the law or by me was anyone's guess.

I went straight to the kitchen when I got back to the brothel because I was starving. I never ate when I was in the Trulos District. I only spoke when I had to because I wasn't all that confident in my fake accent. Beck was just finishing up, but stayed to talk to me.

"I heard some arsehole assaulted Rowena this morning."

"Right in front of me. Guttertown might not have his fancy education, but we aren't that stupid."

"Right? They don't even *know* my aunt was giving you serial killer lessons as a kid and Guttertown knows better than to mess with Rowena."

"I'm not a serial killer."

"Oh, Ronan and I were with Keeva earlier. Ronan is going to be painting murals on the wall and I had about a million questions for my aunt. She smacked me upside the head when I said serial killer instead of assassin. Fair warning, you aren't my aunt. If you hit me, I *will* hit you back."

"That could be nice. I had a lot of fun the last time we hit each other," I said, winking at Beck.

"It was fun. I asked Keeva to teach me what you do, and she told me I didn't have the constitution to be an assassin. It was insulting."

"There's a difference between being a warrior and slitting a man's throat. You've never killed before. Honestly, I don't want you doing that any more than Keeva does."

I was glad Keeva told him no. Beck could kill a man with his fists if he wanted to, but Panas trained him not to unless he had no other choice. The Madame raised him to use his wits and Beck grew into a caring, gentle man. Beck was the one the girls talked to after a man hurt them. Beck helped them with their trauma and I snuck into the men's houses and killed them.

We had designated roles here and I don't think anyone wanted Beck to change a thing about himself.

"It just seems like I could help the girls more if I did that."

"You *are* helping the girls, dumbass. Me killing them just solves the problem of them coming back here and I pass their secret gold stashes along. I obviously can't tell them I'm doing that. That's where you come in. You talk to them about what happened and reassure them that those men were total shits, but there are still good ones out there. That's not me, but it's definitely you."

Because seriously, I was beyond damaged. I knew that. I'd

never make anyone a proper partner and if Momma ever got grandkids to spoil, they would be from Rowena. Because I was going to make damned sure she never ended up like me.

"Ah, Neco. You're one of the good ones, even if one of your hobbies is slitting the throats of abusive men. When are you going to do it?"

"Three days. The Trulos District is having some fucking festival. Too many people around."

"Good."

Yes. Good. That man touched my sister and deserved everything he had coming to him.

LUCY

We were getting mobbed every night because of the Bloody Marys. Ollie and I ended up posting a job to keep up with the demand. We needed someone to work the tavern, and we needed help in the kitchen. Hopefully, Mom would be able to help us soon, but right now, I wouldn't let her work no matter how much she argued with me.

We were doing well money-wise. We had more than enough to pay extra employees and I was socking money aside to invest in the tavern, pay for all the tomatoes we would need, and set some aside for emergencies. Right now, the emergency was Mom.

Ollie was interviewing people before the tavern opened. He was a much better judge of people than I was. He'd be able to tell if someone just wanted free booze and would be lazy or if they would be a hard worker. I could admit that. Ollie was better at people than I was.

I was on my way to find Athan and Tarja to see if they needed anything from me. They were just leaving their shop when I found them.

"Hey, Lance. How's your mom?"

"The herbs are helping a little, but I don't think they are treating the underlying issue. The tavern is doing really well. Is there anything you need to get a cure going?"

"We actually have a lead. Come inside. No one can hear this."

I didn't think any of this would be covert, but I followed them inside, anyway.

"We were gathering herbs with Ilyn and came across a banished Theran."

Earth shifters. They turned into any animal associated with land. Some of them were fearsome beasts. We met one in the woods once. She was around our age. We ended up playing for hours before she had to go back. I always wondered what happened to her.

The Barons painted them as dangerous savages who wanted to wipe humans out, but if you didn't fuck with them, they didn't bother you. I had a lot of fun playing with her. I wasn't worried about one attacking Ilyn, Athan, and Tarja because they were healers and didn't mean anyone harm.

"What'd he get banished for?"

Because that was important.

"The king banished him. He was the bodyguard to the Theran prince. The prince was playing in the woods and got murdered by humans. Basselt found the prince full of arrows and no one around him to avenge him. He brought his body home. The king was devastated and banished Basselt for not protecting his son. Basselt said they banish rather than hang people in the tribes because banishment is so much worse."

"Did they kill the prince because he was Theran or because they didn't know he was Theran?"

Because honestly, you couldn't tell the difference. It was why humans had their territory and the shifters had theirs. We didn't go into shifter land and when they came into ours, they were wearing people faces. You could always tell they were shifters by the robes they wore and the color of those robes let you know if they were Farkhi, Theran, or Tark.

You could also generally tell by looking at them, though the Farkhi could pass as a Jagged Key Isle person and the Theran could mostly pass for humans. I'd never seen a Tark, but from what I understood, no one in Nestran looked like them. They were water shifters, and I didn't know anyone who had laid eyes on one of them before because they were either on their lands or in the water.

"It could be either or. Basselt said the prince was curious about the Festival of Lights near the palace and slipped away from him. No one truly knows who did it and why," Athan said.

"Since the Theran won't have him, none of the tribes will. Basselt said death would have been preferable to banishment, but the shifters have their own religion. His gods would look unfavorably on him taking his own life, but shifters don't do well when they are isolated from people. His wife shunned him and refused to leave with him. He lost his entire family. I honestly think he was just happy to have someone to talk to," Tarja said.

"The shifters have healers, too. Basselt wasn't one, but his wife was. He knows herbs and remedies that we don't, including some for infection that have been curing the shifters *without* the Baron's fancy equipment."

"Did he tell you?"

Because that could cure Mom. I'd give him whatever he wanted.

"He wants to, but he's scared. Basselt is tired of being alone. Guttertown hates the Barons. We have no problem with the shifters. He's been hiding in the woods long enough to have figured that out. He's Theran, so with a haircut and different clothes, he could blend in with us because we can't scent that he's not human like the shifters could.

"He could be around people again and frankly, I don't

think Guttertown would even give a shit if they knew. They'd probably help him hide from the Barons. Basselt is afraid of the Barons, but he's also afraid of the Theran. He shifts into a wolf and they named him a lone wolf when he was banished. He thinks they might react badly if he changes the rules of his banishment by taking up with the humans. Basselt also said some of them hate *all* humans because they've never met one and wouldn't want him sharing any kind of remedy that would heal them."

"Guttertown is for the outcasts. I think we'd welcome him and protect him. I can even give him a job and train him. We're hiring two positions at the tavern. I could put him in the kitchen where there's less of a chance of him getting exposed. I'd pay him so he could afford a house in Guttertown and he could be around people. He could save lives here. Not just Mom, but all of us."

"We told him if he had skills, he'd probably have no problem finding someone to give him work. Like I said, he worried about the Theran retaliating, not just against him, but everyone in Guttertown if he tries this. The Barons are looking for any excuse to get into another war with the shifters. They don't give a shit about Guttertown, but they'd say the shifters broke the treaty they already broke and start conscripting men.

"He said he needed to think about it. He said he would do some kind of Theran thing to commune with nature and see what the best path forward would be. Basselt said he'd meet us in the woods where we were gathering herbs when he made his decision. He also said he'd find us. If he didn't want to be found, it would be impossible to locate him."

"We specifically asked about your mom. He said he knows how to treat it and what he would need grows in and near Guttertown, but some of it won't be ready to harvest for the remedy for a few weeks."

Ugh. Weeks I wasn't sure Mom had.

"When you see him again, tell him he has a job in the kitchen in my tavern if he decides to make Guttertown his new tribe."

I wanted Mom cured more than anything, but I was also looking at the big picture. Basselt could teach Athan and Tarja new remedies and it would help all of us. It might prevent future generations of kids like me from ever having to go to their fathers just because their mom got sick and Guttertown didn't have the means to treat them.

Hopefully, Basselt decided to come work for me and Mom could hold on that long.

OLIVER

I knew we needed the help because holy fuck, those Bloody Marys were popular and I had no doubt when Lucy had her infusion just right, it would be just as popular. We had a lot of people who came in to apply for the job posting, but not all of them were right for the job.

Some of them came because they were under the impression that working in a tavern was going to be easier than what they were currently doing. It wasn't working under the sun and getting filthy, but it was still strenuous work. We had several drinks and food. You had to keep track of who wanted what and then you had to carry it out without spilling it on yourself or customers.

And it wasn't just all of that. We needed a certain kind of disposition. The tavern and the brothel were completely different businesses, but we had a few things in common. I had to pretend to like and flirt with people I couldn't stand. My friends talked about me and my secrets, but that was just part of being a bartender.

I was an uninterested party to get advice from, someone who helped mend relationships, I flirted if I thought someone was feeling down and needed a pick me up, and I pretended not to be uncomfortable when people took flirting with me a little too far.

That was just part of working in the tavern. Ronan wasn't just our friend. He was good at all of that, so we happily let him work when he needed money. What we needed was the full package, and I didn't get anyone for front of house who had that.

I had plenty of people who knew their way around a kitchen, but they weren't right, either. We were offering generous wages, but they wanted free drinks. Which I might have negotiated when they *weren't* working, but they wanted all the free alcohol while they were running the kitchen.

Which was a no for me even without talking to Lucy or Caitrin. That was one of Caitrin's hard rules when she started training Lucy and me to eventually run the tavern. We could either be drinking or working, but we couldn't do both. If she caught us drinking when we were supposed to be working, she would kick us out of the tavern without pay until we were sober and agreed to the rules. Lucy and I never broke that one because we agreed with it.

Lance had always taken the business seriously, and I finally found out it was because Lance was Lucy and never wanted to meet her father. I took it seriously because the tavern used to be my parents'. It was my legacy.

I didn't have a single person come in that I'd actually trust with our baby. Lucy came back in and told me she made a job offer to someone she hadn't even met. Honestly, it sounded like a good fit. Basselt would be motivated to make this work and maybe he could teach us some Theran recipes and we could just pretend they weren't when we served them.

"We didn't have a single man or woman come in that would make a good tavern wench."

"I hate that term," Lucy said.

"That's why I reclaimed it. A man can be a tavern wench, too, if he plays it right."

"Isn't the male version a swain?"

"Not if they want to work in *this* tavern. We're all wenches, even me."

"*I'm* not a wench, Ollie."

"When you're slinging drinks instead of working in the basement, you sometimes channel your inner wench. Own it."

"Don't make me hit you."

"Only a wench would say that."

Before Lucy could assault me and I knew she was about to, an absolutely stunning girl breezed into the tavern. She was squeezed into a corset and walked straight up to us. She struck a sassy, little pose and glared at us. If Autar was here, he already would have asked her to marry him and from the looks of her, gotten a swift kick to the nuts. *She* had tavern wench potential, but I needed to know more.

"So, you know my sister, Lethia."

Yes, we did. As soon as she could, she happily walked into the brothel and demanded a job. Lethia was one of the girls who did it because she chose to and she always had entertaining stories about her work. That meant this was her younger sister, Sabina, who I hadn't realized was all grown up now.

"Is Lethia in trouble?" Lucy asked.

"Fuck no. She's legendary. She's my reference. I'm here for a job. I know how things work. She taught me how to get *anything* I wanted with a little smile and flirt. I don't like fucking guys, so I won't fuck you for this job. I much prefer women. But you'd be stupid not to hire me. Lethia taught me everything she knows about managing drunk men just in case."

Ah, fuck. Sabina might actually be perfect for this if she could keep orders straight, not spill anything, and could stay sober. I liked poking Lucy because I secretly liked it when she hit me. We were different in a ton of ways, but we were *always* on the same page when it came to the tavern. We didn't need to go have some secret meeting in the basement over this.

"We don't want you to fuck us for the job. We're actually fucking each other," Lucy said.

That was the first time she'd said to anyone we were together like that. I wasn't sure if she wanted anyone to know, but I got it. Sabina was used to Lethia's stories where men just wanted sex. Everyone thought Lucy was Lance. Lucy was letting her know we didn't just want sex from her.

"Thoroughly," I said. "How are you at keeping orders straight and carrying drinks out?"

"I've never done it before, but I think I'd be good at it. I was at the top of my class in school. I know it doesn't say much since it was Guttertown school, but I was."

"Sabina, I know Lethia told you what drunk men are like, but have you actually been around them? They will grope you and you can definitely put them in their place. I'd never tell you that you can't, but it has to be done a certain way," Lucy said.

Yeah, because some arseholes got violent if they didn't like how women asked them not to grab them without their permission.

"Oh, I know. I've been dealing with that since I was fourteen. It was why Lethia helped me."

I was guessing some of the men who groped Sabina got their throats slit in the middle of the night by a one-eyed assassin, but no one in this room could know that.

"I think it's a good fit. We can start training you tonight. We're going to be hiring someone for the kitchen, but I don't know if the person I've picked has accepted the job yet," Lucy said.

"We've got food and bread every night. It's generally stew. There are three drinks available and we're working on four. People can buy ale, whiskey, or our new Bloody Mary. It's not really complicated, but when you've got a tavern full of drunk people and a large table yelling their orders, it can be difficult to keep up with because it gets loud in here."

"I can do it. And I'll keep doing it, but I hope one day, you'll let me sing in the tavern. It's what I've always wanted to do and I'm good at it. There's just no place to perform in Guttertown."

I looked over at Lucy and she gave me a brief nod. The Whispering Raven was expanding. We were bringing new drinks to Guttertown, but all of us wanted Guttertown to be more than it was. In the Trulos District, you could pay money just to watch someone perform and performing was their job. We didn't have that in Guttertown and we *should*. We had plenty of talented people.

"Sing for us now," I said.

"Without my girlfriends? One plays the lute and the other bangs on a pan because we don't have real drums. But we're good, I promise."

I looked at Lucy again. Lucy and Catrin handled the book-keeping. I knew we were doing well, but if we hired Sabina and her girlfriends to play the tavern, we'd still need to pay someone to take orders and run them out. We still needed to get Caitrin healed. Lucy had a plan for that, but it was anyone's guess if Basselt would come live in Guttertown. There was also the issue of Lucy squirreling enough money away to never need to go to her father.

"Bring them and play tonight. If you're a hit, you can continue to sing at the tavern. If not, you can work here slinging drinks. Happy people drink more and Guttertown needs some joy. You'd honestly be perfect for slinging drinks, too, so if you know someone who would be a good fit, send them our way."

"I actually do. She's one of my school friends and her mom forced her into an apprenticeship at the dressmaker. She hates it, but her mom was just thinking about her future. I think her mom would accept it if she had another job lined up that wasn't the brothel. Mira's mom absolutely didn't want her working there."

"Send her and we'll interview her," I said. "We'll see you tonight."

After she left, I turned to Lucy.

"Can we afford all that and still keep you away from your father?"

"I'm pretty sure we can, but Sabina is gorgeous. She's sassy and I can just tell she knows how to work a crowd. If she's a talented singer, too, that'll bring more business. We get overflow from the brothel when men outside of Guttertown visit. Some of them have never set foot in here because they think we're serving swill. If we can get them through the doors because they hear Sabina and her girlfriends performing, they'll eventually realize we're not. We may get repeat customers and some private orders like Leodos and his whiskey."

"Those men are insufferable," I moaned.

"Their money isn't. We can lie and charged them more like the Madame does unless we like them like Leodos."

I grabbed Lucy and kissed her.

"That's why you're the brains of the tavern."

LUCY

I tried to be kind, but I couldn't really afford that when it came to my business. I wasn't being kind to Sabina. Well, I was. Her passion was singing and there was no place to really do that outside of her home in Guttertown. I meant what I said to Ollie. The expense in paying her and her friends was a gamble, but it had the potential to bring in new customers.

Leodos loved our whiskey. He special-ordered it from us and paid us handsomely for it. He'd shared it with people in the palace, but they thought he was fucking with them when he said it came from Guttertown, so they never showed up and ordered from us. It was a little insulting. They knew he was banished to Guttertown for a little while, but they thought he was just keeping his whiskey maker secret for some weird reason.

I'd never understand rich people.

But if they walked through the doors of the Whispering Raven because they caught Sabina singing as they were leaving the brothel? They'd know for sure our shit was good and we might get more special orders.

Of course, all of this was hinging on Sabina not being totally tone deaf.

She showed up with her friends when she said she would. Ollie and I had cleared a corner for her. She came with three other girls around her age and walked up to Ollie and me with a pretty girl who dyed her hair red. No one had naturally red hair except the old school Tempris before they started mixing with humans.

People dyed their hair red because Princess Esylle was supposed to be the most beautiful woman in all of Nestran and she was Tempris. I'd never seen her and probably never would, but I heard her hair was black. Still, red hair was wildly popular with the men who thought they could tame a Tempris woman, even if that woman was completely human and colored her hair with herbs.

"This is my friend, Mira, who I said would be good for working the tavern while we sing."

Mira batted her eyelashes at me. I was used to having people flirt with me.

"No need for that," I said. "We're about to get busy. I'll give you a trial tonight to see how you do and we'll go from there."

"I told you he was fucking Ollie," Sabina hissed.

Mira just shrugged.

"Couldn't hurt."

I ran through what we carried, what we were serving tonight, where the kitchen was, and how to take orders. Mira asked a few questions, but said she got it. And then we were off. Everyone was getting off of work and spilling into the tavern.

Sabina set up with her girls to sing and when she opened her mouth, I just stood there for a moment. The entire tavern did. She was enchanting. She had a deep, throaty voice and Sabina wove an entire spell over the tavern. We all just stood and stared for her song.

For the next song, Sabina went into something a little more rousing and the spell was broken. We were packed and my idea worked. A few merchants wandered over from the brothel when they heard her. I threatened to kick them out if they didn't order something and they were surprised at the quality of our spirits.

I was pretty sure we netted a few new regulars and maybe some special orders soon. I didn't notice any problems from Mira. No one was complaining and there was no crashing like something got spilled. That was a good sign. That meant she was working out.

If she liked the work, she could be our new tavern wench, even if I *loathed* that term. We needed more kitchen help because about an hour before call, we couldn't make Bloody Marys again. If we had someone in the kitchen to keep up with the demand, that wouldn't be a problem.

Ollie said everyone he interviewed was a disaster. Hopefully, Basselt would come through. By the end of the night, we were exhausted. I paid the girls for their work and gave them all a shot of whiskey as we sat at the bar with our feet up.

"That was exhausting, but a lot of fun," Mira said.

"You!" Ollie said, pointing at Sabina.

"Me?"

"I think Ollie was trying to say 'damn, girl. You are really good at singing.' The rest of you are amazing as well. Would you have even come in here and asked to sing if I hadn't posted the job?"

"It didn't seem like a possibility before. Everyone in Guttertown is broke. But you posted the job like you have a bit of extra money."

"We do, but it was the three of you that brought in even more," Ollie said.

"True. I'm pretty sure we're going to get some special orders from merchants soon. Mira, you caught on really quickly. I'm going to need you to work with just Ollie in a few days so I can make more whiskey and vodka."

"No problem. How is your mom?"

"About the same. The herbs are keeping things from getting worse, but she's not getting better. We've got a lead on someone for the kitchen who might be able to cure her, but he's unsure and what he needs isn't going to bloom right away."

"If you need anything, let us know."

"Thanks."

The girls left, and I was alone with Ollie.

"Well, that was a success. One of the merchants asked at the bar if we were the place Leodos was getting his whiskey."

"Really?"

"Yeah. I guess those fuckers finally realized he wasn't lying. You were right. A few of them might be special ordering soon."

Good. We weren't desperate for cash and I had a plan for Mom, but I really didn't want to have to contact my father ever.

BECK

We liked giving Ronan a hard time for wanting Ollie to tell him everyone's business, but we all loved hearing it. For instance, I was *fascinated* with Neco's side hobby. He was going to be killing the man who hurt Rowena tonight. Keeva and Neco were right. I didn't think I could kill someone who wasn't actively trying to kill me, but I wanted all the details when Neco did it.

Lucy and Ollie were trying out something new at the Whispering Raven. They had Lethia's sister and her friends making music. They started two nights ago, and they were already a hit for us and the tavern. Our regulars wandered over, eventually realized the drinks there were good, and then they went home and talked about it.

Some of the men who thought they were too good to pay for sex came to watch Sabina sing, got a little drunk and turned on because Sabina and her girlfriends were gorgeous, and surprise! They walked next door and paid for sex. The

Trulos District was paying both businesses handsomely, but also, some of the merchant workers who weren't as rich had also shown up.

I should have been sleeping. Everyone else was, but I was waiting for Neco. He strolled in like he'd just been taking a carefree walk in the moonlight and didn't have a single drop of blood on him. He was dressed in all black, but he always was. Fucker didn't even have a cloak on to disguise his face.

"How'd it go?" I asked.

"Not here," Neco said, cocking his head towards his bedroom.

I followed him and I had so many questions. Neco was pretty distinctive. He was giant, and he wore an eyepatch. I had no idea how he was slipping in and out of the Trulos District without getting caught. Neco sprawled on his bed with his hands behind his head and he had no right to look that sexy. Neco and me couldn't happen again. Lucy wouldn't like it.

"How do you get in and out of the Trulos District without your face covered?"

"By *not* covering my face. I look like I'm not hiding shit. One of the tricks to not getting caught is not looking like you're up to something. Keeva taught me to fake the accent. I'm terrible at it, but no one has noticed yet. The Barons can't keep track of their men and they don't bother learning names unless they consider them important. If someone asks what I'm doing, I name drop my father and say I'm on business for him. They let me go about my way. That deadbeat piece of shit might as well be useful for *something*."

Fascinating.

"Is he dead?"

"As dead as they come. The interloper struck while I was there. He didn't hit the Trulos District this time. I have to pass through Lower Cutwart to get home. They are poor, but not Guttertown poor. He butchered a family there. Those people have slightly more than we do, but compared to the rest of Nestran, they have nothing. There's no reason to hunt there unless you're a psycho doing it for kicks."

Shit. Lower Cutwart bordered Guttertown to the West. It was about the only border the humans wanted to share with us. It was shifter territory North and South and the ocean to the East. Lower Cutwart was about as far as we could go without being spat on or accused of criminal mischief, but they didn't like us that much, either. I guess Lower Cutwart folks consoled themselves at night by saying at least they didn't live in Guttertown.

"Did you find out anything about the victims?"

"Some of the town folks said the family had a teenage girl who was quite beautiful. She was getting a lot of marriage prospects. Even some of the Baron's sons were interested in her. The Baron's daughters can't marry down, but they'll make exceptions for the boys if the girl is pretty enough. They treat the women like property. They said this girl was pretty enough to have gotten that exception. She's dead along with the rest of her family and they said whoever did it butchered them."

"Sounds like a clue."

"Could be. The only way I'm going to get information about the other victims is to get Old Man Aimes drunk and even drunk, he's a sly bastard. He's going to want to know why I'm so curious. It'll look suspicious."

"You could always ask Ollie. That goofy fucker has a way of getting everyone to spill their guts."

I said that, but Ollie wasn't a goofy fucker. He used that pretty face and his position at the tavern to extract information. He was also pretty cunning. He could piece together tidbits from one side of a tall tale and get the actual story. Ollie was a lot smarter than we gave him credit for.

"I'm pretty sure the teenage girl is important. I was going to go back tomorrow and ask around. I stayed in the shadows because everything was still fresh. Want to come with me?"

"Um, yes?"

Because I might be fascinated with Neco and Keeva being assassins, but I was pretty sure I didn't actually want to kill anyone who wasn't trying to kill me. Stopping a serial killer who was butchering entire families?

That actually sounded like a lot of fun.

LUCY

Business was booming and Mom wasn't doing great. She was having trouble catching her breath and while she wasn't coughing up more blood, she was still doing it. I was scared to death and trying not to show it. She kept trying to come and work and I kept telling her she couldn't. She approved of what I was doing with the tavern. I was pretty sure she was bored.

The girls were brilliant. I didn't have many girlfriends. I couldn't tell them I was Lucy, but I was having fun with them. We paid them well, so they were motivated to help out. They knew Mom was sick, and I was hoping to hire someone to work in the kitchen who could possibly cure her. I also let them put a hat out while they were singing so they could busk. If someone wanted to toss them a coin, they could.

They were getting all kinds of fans from all over Nestran and so was the Whispering Raven because we had quality shit. There was just one last thing that needed to fall into place and that happened in the morning.

Athan and Tarja walked into the tavern with a blond man with bright-green eyes. He was dressed like he was from

Guttertown, but I knew he was Theran. He could pass for human but because they had given me a hint about Basselt, I was pretty sure he'd finally decided to give us a try. He was older, probably around Mom's age or a few years older than her.

"Hi!" I said, marching over and sticking my hand out. "I'm Lance."

Basselt just cocked an eyebrow at me.

"Okay, *Lance*," he drawled, taking my hand. "If you'll have me, I'll take the job. You can clearly keep secrets."

Basselt gave me a knowing look. He knew. He knew I was a girl. How the actual fuck? He didn't want to know anything about the job. It was my hidden vagina that did it for him.

"How?"

Because seriously, how? No one had figured it out. Ollie only managed because I bled through my pants. There was no way. Basselt just tapped his nose.

"Extra senses."

"Do I stink?"

"No, but I don't think you want me to answer anything else in front of Tarja and Athan."

Nope. No, I didn't. Fucking Hell. The Theran could just scent I wasn't male. That was a neat trick. It was also dangerous.

"Now that Basselt is here and is agreeing to help, we want to get him around your mom," Athan said.

"I don't know what secret he scented out, but the shifters don't just use their nose for that. They can scent sickness, too. Basselt should be able to give us a better diagnosis for Caitrin and let us know where to go from here."

"Seriously?"

Basselt bowed his head.

"I'm not a healer. My wife was, but I picked up on some of it. If it's an infection, I know what that smells like. Is your mother going to be okay with this?"

That was a thing about Mom. Even if she wasn't okay with something, she'd pretend like she was until she got me alone. She'd be fine with Basselt even if he wasn't here to help her and she'd be totally okay with him working in the tavern.

"She'll be okay. Come up."

They all followed me upstairs. Mom was napping on the couch, so I gently woke her. She groaned and started coughing.

"It's an infection," Basselt said. "She's got some nasty fluid in her lungs. I can smell it from here."

"Excuse me, but I *do not* stink," Mom snapped.

"Mom, Basselt is Theran. He was banished for something that wasn't his fault. He's going to be working in the kitchen and he's got an idea how to cure you. His wife was a healer. He's not saying you stink. He's got extra senses we don't have."

"Hrpmh. I suppose he can look at me."

Was Mom...into Basselt? I might not get to be Lucy much, but I'd played in the brothel as a kid. Mom and Basselt were looking at each other like they were into each other. Mom would have been considered off limits by Guttertown men because of my father. They knew if he ever wanted to come back, they'd have to give her up. Basselt would need that explained to him if he wanted to proceed.

"I can do it from here. Your lungs have nasty fluid in them. It's what's causing all of this. I told Athan and Tarja I know the remedy, but I can't make it yet. The plant I need grows near here, but it's not ready to be harvested yet. You just make a tea with it and some ginger and honey. Drink it for a few days and it'll clear it right up. But the plant isn't ready right now. Can you hold on?"

"I'm not going to die yet."

"Is there something you can give her that will help in the meantime?" I asked.

"Nothing that Athan and Tarja aren't already doing.

There's a lot of overlap between what my people do and what the humans do. Their treatment is excellent. Back in the Theran village, they'd already have the plant dried and stored for when it's in its dormant season, but I'm not welcome there."

"What'd you do?" Mom asked.

"Didn't watch an eight-year-old prince close enough. He shifted and tried to see the Festival of Lights. He got murdered by humans. It's my biggest regret in life."

"I raised an eight-year-old. You can be right on top of them and they'll still sneak off and get into trouble. You didn't kill him. Humans did. Forgive yourself, even if the Theran can't."

Basselt bowed his head.

"Logically, I know that, but I had one job. They take banishment seriously. I'll never be forgiven or welcomed back by them. The Theran heir died in my care."

"Then, welcome to Guttertown. We're a town of misfits. I doubt they'd even care that you're Theran."

"The Theran would care that I'm here, so it's best we keep that as much a secret as Lance's."

Mom narrowed her eyes at Basselt and I could tell the momma bear was about to come out. She would drag herself out of bed coughing up blood to beat the shit out of this man if she thought he would expose me to my father.

"Super nose," I said. "He let me know that he knew without exposing me to Athan and Tarja. We can trust him."

Basselt just shrugged.

"I figure he has his reasons. It's not my business."

That was kind of nice. He knew I was pretending to be a man because he could scent I was female and Basselt didn't give the slightest fuck why. He didn't assume everyone knew, but were just humoring me. Basselt basically just subtly let me know that he knew, and that it meant he could trust me. I appreciated it.

"You will protect that secret with your life," Mom snarled.

"He's just a kid. I'm not letting another one get hurt under my watch."

I was twenty, but okay.

"Let me show you the kitchen and give you a walk-through of how we run things. We have a new drink and I'll have to teach you how to make the base. There's no drinking in the kitchen. You can drink all you want when you aren't working, but not when we need you functioning. Is that going to be a problem?"

Basselt smirked at me. It was the first time I'd seen him smile since he came in. If he was amused because he knew I was a girl and was bossing him around, he was going to have a serious problem working here. I needed him to realize Mom was the owner of this tavern until she officially signed it over to Ollie and me, so no matter which way he sliced it, he'd be taking orders from a woman.

"You're talking to the former bodyguard of the Theran heir. You don't have to lecture me about staying sober at work. It was part of my training before I got on the job. I would take working in your kitchen as seriously as I did protecting my charge. I wouldn't mess up like I did before."

I waited until we were alone in the kitchen. I didn't know the first thing about shifter culture, but I knew how things were outside of Guttertown. I got that his smirk was because I was lecturing him not to drink in the kitchen when he'd literally been a bodyguard to a prince. Thing was, I didn't know how long he'd been banished and that had to change him. I had every right to bring it up.

"Listen, I'm not trying to sound like an ignorant human who knows absolutely nothing about your culture, but are you going to have a problem working for me now that you know the truth? Because my mom is actually the owner, so you'd have to answer to both of us."

Basselt let out a belly laugh.

"I'm not laughing *at* you, I promise. I'm just thinking what a fierce Theran you'd make. To answer your question, we aren't like humans at all in that respect. The animal you shift into is more important than what's in your pants and there's an entire process that I find a little stupid for assigning that animal. We can shift into anything we want within our element until our tenth birthday. The king or queen chooses the animal we'll be stuck with for the rest of our lives and it's generally associated with what job you'll have.

"So, we've got women who are fierce warriors and men who clean and tend to people's houses. The last two generations seem to be all men, but if the firstborn is a girl, she'll rule her tribe and take a consort. Our god and creator is a woman. We pray and light incense for her return every day. I know it's not the same among humans and I find that very stupid because a woman can lead an army just as well as a man can, but trust me, I have no problem working under two strong women, even if everyone thinks you're a man."

I owed it to him since he knew my dirty secrets. I explained everything with the Guttertown Argent kids and what would happen to me if I eventually needed my father for anything and he found out I was a woman. Basselt just looked at me sadly.

"If I could force nature to hurry up, I would."

So would I. Mom's life and my freedom depended on it.

NECO

Lower Cutwart liked to pretend they were better than Guttertown, but they really weren't. They were dirtier, for one. The Jagged Key Isles people that came over brought their love of bathing with them and most of us adopted it. Sometimes, it was cold baths, but we all took them pretty frequently. We had easier access to water than Lower Cutwart, so that probably had something to do with it.

Beck and I were walking about questioning people. It was nice. I usually worked alone, but it was nice to have a partner. Most of these people knew I was from Guttertown, so I wasn't faking the accent. Beck was clearly from the Jagged Key Isles. They weren't outright rude because we could clearly smash their faces in, but they were still snotty little bitches.

Except for the ones who were flirting with us. We'd moved on to talking to the friends of the girl who was murdered. I didn't know why, but I could just tell she was a clue.

"So, how'd you lose your eye," the girl giggled, stroking my arm.

This girl had to be sixteen, tops. I liked my women older. I wouldn't have gone there no matter what, and I didn't particularly like small talk. I definitely didn't like people touching me. There were only a few people on this Earth that I didn't want to murder when they touched me and she wasn't one of them.

Beck noticed right away and swooped in to save me. I appreciated it because it felt like bugs were crawling on my skin when I got unwanted touches. Beck usually walked around shirtless when it was warm out and it was finally starting to get there. He flexed his chest and biceps and the three girls practically swooned. I wasn't even mad they forgot all about me. I wanted them to.

"Tell us about Elsbeth," Beck said. "Would anyone want to hurt her?"

They all exchanged looks like they didn't want to say something. The rest of Nestran thought if you spoke ill of the dead, their spirit would come back and curse you, but Gutter-town knew that wasn't true. We trash talked the dead all the time. We knew damned well if shitty things happened, it was the living Barons doing it, so we talked shit about the dead ones all the time. That was just idiotic talk for people who didn't see things for what they were.

"It's okay. Say what you will. We're trying to catch who did this. Elsbeth's spirit will rest and not curse you for what-ever you say if it helps catch her killer," Beck purred.

Yeah, Beck had this way of doing this deep sexy thing with his voice. It could get anyone to do anything. All three girls giggled again and practically melted in their seats. Would Rowena eventually get like this? Because right now, she was ten and definitely more about punching boys in the dick than flirting with them.

I wouldn't be ready for it if Rowena got like this with older men.

"So, Elsbeth really liked boys and boys really liked Elsbeth. She was stringing a few of them along. Elsbeth didn't want to stay in Lower Cutwart, so she was juggling a few sons of merchants and two Barons' sons. The merchant boys knew about each other and the Baron heirs knew about each other, but I don't think the merchants and the Barons knew they were competing against each other."

"But it doesn't make sense any of them would go after Elsbeth and her family. You don't know how pretty she was. She also had five brothers and good hips. Elsbeth would have had many attractive sons. The merchants couldn't have gone after the Barons and the Barons would have just killed the merchants."

The little Baron crotch fruit would have gotten off Scot free. I suppose one of the merchants could have decided if they couldn't have Elsbeth, then no one could, but merchants didn't typically try to piss off the Barons. They were too busy licking their boots. It was more than likely they would have just stepped aside when they found a Baron heir was involved.

Beck and I excused ourselves. We'd gotten all we could get out of them and I didn't want them to get any more ideas about touching me. I usually put people in their place when they touched me without my permission, but these were just young girls and we might need to talk to them again.

Beck was on the same wavelength as me. We needed more information about the other victims first.

"Elsbeth and her beauty *might* be completely unrelated or it could be the very reason her family got butchered," Beck said. "Trevils would be reporting back to the Barons. Their sons would be there so they can train to be future arseholes. It could be a copycat. One of them could have done it to piggyback on the current killings."

"I suppose it's possible," I said. "But not likely. In the Jagged Key Isles, an assassin is a legitimate job. You can apprentice with them. That kind of thing is illegal in Nestran, but your ancestors passed down the training until it got to Keeva and she taught me.

"I have the tools and skills to break into a house without

being seen. A mini-Baron wouldn't have that. He probably wouldn't know the first thing about breaking into a house. If he knocked and they let him in, someone would have seen. The houses in Lower Cutwart are right on top of each other. The fact that no one saw anything speaks to a certain level of skill that no one is going to have on their first kill."

"It's fucked up that you know that."

I just shrugged and winked at Beck.

"What does it say about you that you're so fascinated by it?"

"Obviously, I'm not going to think too hard about that, arsehole."

"So, we're going to have to rope Ollie into this. He has a way with people and he controls most of the booze in Guttertown. Can you manage that without fucking Lance ruining it?"

"Lance knows the Blight is someone in Guttertown, but he's not looking into who it is because he thinks they are doing good work. He would definitely care about this other person butchering innocents. Lance wouldn't fuck that up just because the two of you don't get along."

I snorted.

"Lance would rat me out to Inspector Trevils in a heartbeat."

"No, he wouldn't. I don't even think he hates you. He says it so much because he's trying to convince himself. I don't think *you* hate him, either."

"Shut the fuck up about Lance Argent," I growled.

As far as the subject of Lance Argent went, it was best to avoid that and the man himself entirely.

LUCY

Ollie was up to something. Half the time, when Ollie was up to something, we spent a night in the cells and we couldn't afford to do that with Mom sick and a bunch of new people who barely knew how to run the tavern without us.

"Why are we getting Aimes drunk and asking him about serial killers again? Didn't you lie for him? You need to be as far away from this as possible."

"Okay, so Beck is my boyfriend, and he asked me to poke Aimes for answers, but you're my girlfriend, so I can't keep secrets from you. So, I'm keeping you in the loop. There are two killers. One of them is from Guttertown and he's only killing people who deserve it.

"There's a second one who is butchering entire families, and he even killed in Lower Cutwart. The first one kills men like the second one, so if we can get some details about the investigation and pass them along to the *good* serial killer, he'll take care of the bad one before he makes his way to Guttertown."

"Why are you and Beck hanging out with serial killers again?"

"Well, *technically* he's not a serial killer. He gets really upset if you call him one. He said there's a different between what he does and a serial killer. I'm explaining this wrong."

"You're explaining this pretty terribly, Ollie. I don't like that you and Beck are involved and I certainly don't want to be."

"Okay, so let me explain. You know how the Jagged Key Isle people brought over their culture when they came here? An assassin is a legitimate job over there. People pay them money to kill people and they basically decide if they want to take the job or not. It's supposed to be different from a serial killer."

"Okay, that's worse. You see how that's worse, right?"

"Nah, assassins are more like pest control. It's not this *urge* to kill where they slaughter entire families. They get in, kill their target, and get out. It's a job and if they don't agree with the kill, they don't take it."

It hit me. Was this a test? Ollie had given me a ton of clues. That kind of thing was a massive secret, but so was me being Lucy. I told them all my truth. They could have told me *before* we all had sex. I didn't particularly appreciate the passive-aggressive tests.

"It's Beck, isn't it? Beck is the Blight."

Ollie fell out laughing, and I'd never wanted to punch him in the face more than I did right now.

"Beck is Jagged Key Isles, but he basically thanks the animal for their sacrifice when he kills them for food and he's such a softie, he won't smash bugs. He brings them outside. When they sneak back inside, he scolds them and brings them back out. He'd only kill to defend himself or his loved ones and it would upset the fuck out of him. Beck isn't the Blight. I don't even know if he'd be offended or think it was hilarious you thought it was him. You *know* Beck."

I knew I did. I also spent a long time lying to Beck about who I was. I knew they were all together, and I was on the outside because I had to be. It was lonely a lot of times, but it was how it had to be until I could tell them the truth. They never made me feel left out, but I guess I had a moment of self-doubt where I thought everything I knew about Beck was a lie and they were all in on it.

"You didn't have to laugh at me."

"Yeah, I did. You thought because you kept Lucy from us that Beck kept the Blight from you and that you deserved it. But all you kept from us was what was underneath your clothes. You're still the same mean person who hits me and has brilliant ideas for the tavern whether you're Lance or Lucy."

"I want to hit you for laughing at me," I grumbled.

"That's not really fair. I won't hit you back anymore."

"Because I'm Lucy?"

"Because you're now my girlfriend and I won't. Now, I know the logical portion of your brain needs to hear this. The Blight is from Guttertown and he only kills bad people. The other killer kills indiscriminately and he's moved to Lower Cutwart.

"The Barons aren't going to pressure Trevils to look into it as much if that's his new hunting grounds. If he starts killing in Guttertown, they will just let him because they don't give a shit about us. And you know how this works. If he's anyone important, the Barons won't do anything to him. They'll deliberately point him towards Guttertown and tell him to do his killing away from them. If we get the Blight enough information, he can deal with it."

Ugh. Ollie was right, and he knew exactly what I needed to hear. I still didn't want any of us involved in this. If this blew back on us, it wouldn't be a night in the cells. We'd hang. If they thought any of us were killing people in the Trulos District, they'd punish our families, too.

"You're leaving something out. If it is someone important,

they are going to have to pin it on someone and hang them. It's usually someone they have a problem with but if we're publicly involving ourselves in the investigation, any one of us could be that scapegoat."

"That's why we're talking to Aimes and not Trevils. Aimes will know everything Trevils does because they are old military friends and drinking buddies. Aimes loves to tell stories when he's drinking. You just need to give him a little nudge in the right direction. *You* aren't going to be having that conversation. I'm better at that than you are. You're going to keep the drinks and food coming."

"Fine, because I don't want to risk anyone in Guttertown. But if I noticed Aimes is working you back, I'm putting an end to it."

"That's why we make such an amazing team."

"Is Ronan in on this, too?"

Did everyone know who the Blight was but me? I didn't want to know. I was good at keeping secrets, but I didn't particularly like keeping them. It was too much stress. I was constantly worried about doing or saying the wrong thing and being exposed. Everyone finding out I was really Lucy would have been devastating if I ever needed anything from my father. If I slipped up in front of the wrong person and let them know I was protecting the Blight, it would be fatal.

I didn't want to know.

"Ronan knows who the Blight is, but he's in artist mode at the moment. He's excited about the new project the Madame threw his way. We probably won't see him for a while and the only reason he's remembering to eat is because someone at the brothel threatens to beat his ass."

"We'll also have to go over there and threaten that pretty face because I know how he gets."

"Aimes has been on one of his walkabouts, but he'll be in soon. Hopefully with information."

Ugh. I hated this. If it wasn't Beck, it was probably one of his relatives. Panas, maybe? No. I didn't want to know. I didn't really want to be anywhere near this. Ollie was always dragging me into his shenanigans.

I hoped we didn't hang this time.

OLIVER

S peak of the devil. The man of the hour came in shortly after Lucy had her freak out about getting in bed with a murderer. I was *so* glad she didn't want to know who it was because she'd lose her shit if she found out she was protecting Neco Argent. She wouldn't turn him in, but she'd definitely light my arse on fire.

That could be hot.

As soon as Old Man Aimes came in, I swooped in with a drink and Lucy came by with stew and bread. We didn't need the girls this early. Only Basselt was here in the kitchen. Lucy disappeared to help him. I was still processing that Basselt could just sniff her and figure out she wasn't a boy. That was weird.

"So, any news on the Trulos District murderer? I heard he hit Lower Cutwart a few nights ago. I also heard a rumor there were two different murderers."

"How'd you hear that, boy?"

Fuck. Aimes's watery blue eyes immediately snapped to attention and took me in. He was taking my measure. I just grinned and shrugged. I played it off.

"Trevils was in here talking about this Blight. He said he slips into your house in the dead of night and leaves no evidence. Lower Cutwart is next door. My friends were there when they found the bodies. They said it was really messy and one of the daughters was pretty. It's a shame when a pretty girl dies. Just curious."

"Can you keep a secret?"

"Better than anyone I know."

"There *are* two killers. The Blight started first. Trevils has been looking for him for a while. Trevils is calling the second one The Ghoul."

Oh, man. Beck said Neco was a little ambivalent about his serial-killer name. I hoped he didn't take out Trevils because the Ghoul was so much cooler than The Blight. Also, I'd never say that to Neco because I didn't want my throat slit and he seemed kind of sensitive about being called a serial killer instead of an assassin. It was honestly kind of one of those potato/po-tah-to things, but I wasn't going to have that conversation with him.

"The Ghoul is the one who made Lower Cutwart their hunting ground recently, right? Seems like they are making their way to Guttertown. The Barons will have Trevils stop investigating if he comes here."

"That doesn't mean he's going to stop looking into it. But yeah. The Blight only kills men. No one has figured out how he's picking them or how he's getting into the houses without waking anyone. The Ghoul kills entire families, and he paints skulls on the walls with their blood."

Gross. Neco would never.

"How is he leaving without getting caught? He has to be covered in blood. Even if he's taking the time to take a bath, he'd still have to leave the house covered in blood to fetch the water. The Trulos District has a river that feeds to the ocean, but Lower Cutwart is pretty landlocked. They have a lake, but it's a walk from the town and he'd still be seen covered in blood."

"You'd make a half-decent inspector. We don't know. We're pretty sure the Blight is sneaking into the houses and that's how the rest of the house doesn't know he's there. We don't know how the Ghoul is getting in.

"The people in the house who are old enough appeared to have been gathered in the sitting room. They were picked off, and he chased a few. The kids were in bed at the time. They were all killed in their bedrooms."

"Well, if they were knocking on the front door, someone would have seen them. Especially in Lower Cutwart. And if they were from Guttertown or Lower Cutwart, they would have been kicked off the stoop in the Trulos District," I said.

"All things Trevils has considered. There is one thing all the victims have in common, but it might not mean anything. There was a pretty sixteen-year-old girl among all the Ghoul's victims.

"Like I said, it might not mean anything. She'd be of marrying age, but she'd have no say in who she's married off to. Her father would have the final say and he's going to pick who makes him the most money. There's been six Ghoul murders, and they started in the Trulos District.

"Merchant sons can be ugly as sin inside and out, but men will marry their daughters off to them because of money. There are the outliers who will tell them no because they give a shit, but if the Ghoul is a merchant boy killing because he's getting turned down for marriage, it just wouldn't happen that many times. The sixteen-year-old girl might be completely unimportant. It's just the only connection we can find so far."

Neco would know. I preferred slinging drinks instead of the dark stuff. People came to the Whispering Raven to cut loose and have fun. I liked giving them that. Lucy wanted no part of this because of how dangerous it was. I just didn't like thinking about people getting killed.

Still, Neco might have pulled away, but he was still one of us and we'd protect him.

"Was the bloody skull in every room or just one? I feel like that could be a clue."

"He got creative with the blood in every room. It was a skull in the living room. Most everyone died running from him. There were a few in the halls. He painted a smiling face in the kids rooms. There was one bloody butterfly in every house."

Gross. Neco at least had a code, and he wasn't finger painting with people's blood.

"I feel like the butterfly is important," I said.

"So does Trevils because he's not discussing any theories about it. He doesn't want anyone influencing his ideas, so he never discusses them until he's come up with a theory on his own. Not even with me and I've known him forever. You know, you're pretty good at this. You could make a living at it."

"No way. This shit is too dark for me. I just needed to be reassured it wasn't coming to my backyard. We just hired four new girls. One is slinging drinks and the other three are making music. You should come back tonight and hear them perform. They are talented."

"Oh, I heard about them all the way in the Trulos District. A few of the fancy famous singers there are taking offense at some people saying Guttertown trash has more talent than they do. The whiskey makers are pissed off, too, because they are worried about losing their customers.

"A few of them are trying to replicate your Bloody Mary, but they don't know what spirit you're using or the exact recipe. I checked them out because I thought you and Lucy would want to know. They think all you're capable of brewing is shitty stuff, so they tried to serve everyone tomato soup with their cheapest bourbon in it. I told Trevils he should have arrested them on principle because even without the bourbon, the tomato soup was vile."

Ugh. Lucy was going to be livid. They'd never figure it out unless she shared her vodka recipe with them and she wouldn't.

"Arseholes," I growled.

"I did you a solid. I spread the word that the *real* Bloody Mary couldn't be replicated outside the Whispering Raven and if they wanted to try it, they needed to make the trip to Guttertown."

"Thanks, Aimes."

That was what the rest of Nestran didn't understand. Everything was about money with them. We barely had that in Guttertown, but we understood some things were more valuable. Aimes couldn't do a lot of jobs because of his leg. He did what he could, and we bartered with him.

Lucy and I gave him free food and drink when no one was around to bitch about it because Aimes was a big part of our childhood. He watched us a lot when Caitrin was working late at the tavern. He could have been a total grump who hated children, but he told us fascinating stories and we adored him.

We took care of him now that we were adults because we still liked his stories. Aimes helped us when he could by talking up the tavern.

Aimes helped me in more ways than one. He got me information to help Neco and Guttertown and he brought the tavern some new business.

It was a shame the only person outside of Guttertown who saw what a treasure Aimes is was actively looking into one of my best friend's murder hobby and would see him hang for it.

LUCY

Old Man Aimes wasn't a harmless, doddering drunk. His father was a moron booting him from his army because if his leg. Aimes's strength wasn't in his sword hand. He was a cunning strategist. He could have won any war or skirmish without leaving his chair.

It was why Aimes and Trevils were such good friends. They were both brilliant. Aimes could break into my basement, drink every barrel down there, and still be as cunning as a serpent. Ollie was also smart, and he knew how to play a role. He did it with every single customer he talked to at the tavern. Ollie was a different person to each customer.

For once, I was glad when Aimes left. I didn't want Ollie anywhere near this. Ollie got up and kissed me.

"Hey, can you cover things for a minute?"

Yeah, I could. Basselt took to the kitchen right away. He said in shifter culture, most men knew how to cook and care for a house. He just needed a recipe to follow, and he was good. Ugh. If being able to shift into an animal wasn't cool enough. It sounded like they didn't really subscribe to traditional Nestran gender roles. Maybe I should have been born a shifter.

I told myself I didn't want to know, but I knew Ollie was about to go tell the Blight what Aimes just said. I stuck my head out of the window and watched Ollie walk straight into the brothel. Which meant he *lied* to me. I supposed it could be Panas, but there were only two Jagged Key Isles men who lived in the brothel—Beck and Panas.

If it was Panas, I would have heard about it before now. Panas was a few years older than Mom. It just seemed weird that he would snap and suddenly start killing recently. Beck didn't make sense, either. But I put on a certain face to the public. Beck could, too.

I'd have to think how to approach this and why Ollie lied to me when I asked.

I stomped off to the kitchen. Basselt was plugging away. He had several barrels done already and his stew smelled fantastic. I told him he could try a few recipes of his own when he said he knew how to cook. This would be one of them.

"Oh, gods. What is that? It smells amazing."

"Some wild goat I hunted with potatoes and herbs."

"Thank you. For taking over the hunting. Ollie is juggling the tavern and trying to help out on his uncle's farm. He also sucks at hunting and there's someone who's been stealing rabbits out of my snares. Our stews usually have more potatoes than meat."

"Not anymore, little one. I'm an apex predator. I set some aside and made a meat pie for your mother. She's going to need to keep her strength up until the plant I need finally blooms. Why don't you bring that up to her and make tea with these herbs?"

"Thanks, Basselt. One of the best things we did this moon cycle is hire you."

Ollie wasn't back yet, and this was our slow time. We didn't have anyone in the tavern after Aimes left, so I locked the doors and went upstairs. Mom looked utterly bored. I was pretty sure she'd darned everything that needed to be darned.

"Basselt made this for you. Said you needed to keep your strength up. He made one for me, too, so eat with me."

"This is miserable, Lucy. I have nothing to do."

I removed the cover from the tray Basselt prepared and found something more precious than money in Guttertown. It was a book of Theran stories. He had to have left this for Mom. Ugh. If it were up to me, Mom and Basselt would ride off into the sunset together and basically never think of my father again.

But it was so taboo. There was the shifter-human thing for one. The second was that the Barons basically decided they were going to have a relationship with some Guttertown woman and they couldn't say no. Then the rest of the men in Guttertown basically shunned them because they knew what would happen if that Baron ever came back.

Mom deserved to be happy, and I *liked* Basselt. Maybe it was just me being a girl now that I had three boyfriends. I took a bite out of Basselt's meat pie and nearly died.

"Oh, gods. I'm not trying to pressure you, but I wouldn't say no to Basselt as a stepfather if he cooks like this."

"And I'm not trying to get your hopes up, but he's exactly my type. None of us have to worry about your father coming back because he likes his mistresses young. I'm too old for him now. You're forgetting one major problem. He's a shifter and I'm human. I don't really care, but he might. Plus, he's already married."

"Well, his shifter wife turned her back on him after he got banished and so did the rest of the shifters. I'd say you have a shot."

"Look who got some big breeches now that she finally told her friends she's not a man and that she's in love with them."

"Mom," I moaned, burying my face in my hands.

She must be feeling better if she was poking at me. It was

just the relationship we had. We liked to embarrass each other. She was always a mom to me but she was also my best friend. And then I realized I was horribly mistaken. She wasn't feeling better. We'd officially moved into me breaking her trust and contacting my father.

Mom's whole body seized as she started coughing. She crashed to the floor with blood pouring out of her mouth. I screamed for Basselt, but enhanced hearing must be a shifter thing like their sense of smell. He was already through our door before I'd even finished calling his name. He must have heard the crash.

Basselt immediately rolled Mom on her side.

"I need you to dissolve salt into hot water and bring it to me with something to dribble into her nose. I'll also need any honey you've got in the tavern. It's going to be a little awhile before I have any hope of foraging what I need to fix this. I know *you* don't want to and she doesn't want you to, but this is bad.

"It's up to you whether you want me to try to do what I can until the plant is ready, but it might not be enough. I can try to drain what's in her lungs until I can cure the infection, but until the infection is gone, they will fill again. And if they fill too much, she will die."

Fuck. I was *so* close to fixing this without having to contact my utter shit-stain of a father. I'd only just met Basselt, but there was just something about him that made me trust him. He was telling me the truth, and he wasn't lying to me to make me feel better in this exact moment.

It would have made me feel better now, but if Mom had died when I had time to do what literally no one wanted me to do, I never would have been the same. Basselt spelled it out for me. He'd do his best, but we might not have time.

Mom knew me. She raised me. She was the one who said it was sometimes better to ask for forgiveness than permission, though she hated it when I used that against her.

This time, I'd be doing the one thing she asked me to never do. I'd be losing everything. I'd be conscripted into my father's army and they might eventually find out I wasn't Lance. I'd either hang or get tossed to the brothel. I'd be limited in working in the tavern doing what I loved and I wouldn't see my boyfriends as much anymore.

But Mom would be alive, so it would be worth it.

RONAN

I was grateful Neco and I were cool again, but I didn't realize being in Neco's world as an adult was going to involve so much subterfuge over all the murder. Like, I had a job that paid well that I was very excited about, but Ollie pulled me into Neco's flat to talk about the other serial killer when I could have been painting maidens getting railed by dragons.

Guttertown fables had *nothing* on Jagged Key Isles stories and they told them to children. The stories were raunchy as fuck, but they were also a ton of fun. I was looking forward to painting them on the walls. I *should* be getting my sketches together to show to the Madame.

I wasn't judging Neco for what he did. I could appreciate it in a way. Those people could waltz into Guttertown and murder anyone they liked with no consequences. Neco was just stopping them before it got to that. He was evening the field.

I didn't get the other killer, and I didn't want to. I wanted everything around me to be beautiful and he didn't fit my narrative. Yet, here I was, discussing it with my friends.

Neco really was a psychopath. Hot, but a psychopath.

"The *Ghoul?* Why does he get a better nickname than me?"

"Um, maybe we should be focusing on catching him instead of your monikers?" I said.

"Focus, Neco," Beck said. "Is any of that giving you clues?"

"We need to know which room the butterfly was in. That's going to be how he's picking his victims. It could be the pretty girl and it might not be."

"Yeah, but Aimes told me Trevils isn't talking about that with him yet. We'll have no way of knowing until that happens and I'm not sure if Aimes is going to get squirrelly if I press him again."

"No, you did good. Lance doesn't know, does he?" Neco asked.

We all shared a look. We could probably fix the divide in our friend group by telling Neco Lance was really Lucy. Lucy would never forgive us so that would never happen.

"No, he doesn't. He was actually ready to kick all of our arses because he thought The Blight was Beck."

"What the fuck?" Beck asked.

"And then he wanted to kick my arse for laughing at him."

Lance might be Lucy, but Lucy was a scrappy fighter, and she fought dirty. She could probably kick everyone's arses except for Neco and Beck and that was only because they had training. She could definitely beat the shit out of Ollie and me.

"He would have won," Beck snorted.

"What is happening right now?" Neco asked. "I've got the interloper killing in my territory and now Lance is giving Beck credit for my work?"

"Uh, focus," I said. "I'm pretty sure you don't want anyone correcting Lance."

Seriously? Neco was going to blow everything because he was getting pissy about the whole serial-killer thing. Excuse me, assassin. I could just picture the surly motherfucker in a tavern while someone was ranting about the Blight and going into a long-winded speech about the difference between serial killers and assassins.

And Neco was usually a man of few words.

We didn't have a plan. Neco couldn't take out the Ghoul because he still didn't have enough information. I'd bet he could get it, though. Neco and Beck were working together on this. They'd been in Lower Cutwart asking around. They could do this.

Before we could say anything, the Madame burst into Neco's room in a panic.

"Neco, it's your mom. She's taken a turn for the worse. I've called Athan and Tarja and some of the best healers from my people. I hate to say this to any of the Argent kids, but it might be time to contact your father."

Fuck. Neco loved his mother just as much as he hated his father. With the fire of a thousand suns. Neco was also a trained assassin with a code. His father hurt his mother. I didn't know who his father was, but he would be one of the few people in Nestran that Neco *couldn't* kill.

Neco had restraint and cared about his mom. He could be in the same room as his father without killing him, right?

"I know the two of you had a falling out, but I'm being told Caitrin has also taken a turn for the worst. Lance has also left to ask his father for help."

Fuck! That was the *last* thing we wanted to happen. One of us should have been there to talk Lucy out of it. It wasn't that we thought she couldn't cut it as a soldier or that we'd want nothing to do with her if she worked at the brothel.

It would be that her choice was taken from her. She loved

working at the tavern and she was good at it. Neco's choice would be taken from him, too. Lucy was already gone, but we could help Neco.

"Can it wait a little longer?" Ollie asked. "We just hired someone in the kitchen who knows of a plant that could cure both of them, but it's not ready to harvest yet."

Neco and Lucy had a lot more in common than they'd care to admit. They were both fiercely devoted to their mothers and hated their fathers.

They'd also both ruin their lives if it meant saving their moms. Neco didn't even give us a chance to talk him out of it or hear what the Madame had to say about his mom possibly holding on long enough for this cure.

He was already out the door.

NECO

Fuck my father. I needed his help, but I had conditions. He could take anything he wanted from me, but he was leaving Rowena out of it. If Momma or Rowena needed him again, he'd take a second payment from me. He was never getting his hands anywhere near my baby sister.

No one in Guttertown wanted an Argent kid to have to go to their father for anything. I knew the guys were going to try to talk me out of it, so I left. I didn't know why they were so terrified that Lance had already gone.

I might have complicated feelings towards Lance Argent, but he'd be fine. He was pretty scrawny, but he was fast and could handle himself in a fight. Nestran wasn't at war. The Barons were looking for any excuse to wipe out the shifters, but the shifters weren't taking the bait. The rock from Idric Island near the Jagged Key Isles neutralized their magic and everyone knew that.

The chances of us going to war during my lifetime were slim. Lance was used to dealing with drunk patrons at the tavern. That would be the worst he would be dealing with when he got conscripted. He'd be fine. I didn't know why everyone looked like they were about to shit their pants that he already left.

I'd already sent a pigeon ahead with a message I was asking for an audience. Lance would have done the same. I figured he had a head start and that I'd be waiting for him to get done, but he was sitting on a bench in the hallway of the palace when I got there.

This place was fancy as fuck and it just pissed me off. I knew the king and his daughter were literally powerless against the Barons, but did they know a few miles away in Gutter-town, we didn't even have the books I could see carelessly placed on a table and forgotten?

There were portraits all over the walls of long dead people. If someone in your family died before you were born, you were fucked when it came to knowing what they looked like. You just had to form a picture in your head from descriptions the people who knew them gave you.

Someone went bustling by me with a tray of food. Did they know people went hungry outside these walls? We were basically just trying to survive, and they had people cooking for them and bringing it to them on silver platters. It was fucked up.

And there was no place to sit except next to Lance Argent so I just leaned against the wall and crossed my arms. I wanted to check on Momma, but I was going to have to wait my turn and Lance got here first.

"First of all, fuck you," Lance said. That was basically what he said every time he saw me. "Secondly, please tell me you aren't here because Theda is as bad off as Mom."

I didn't get a chance to answer. What were the odds Momma and Caitrin got the same illness and took a turn at the same time? It was like the gods were fucking with me and thrusting Lance at me during the worst moment of my life. Lance made me feel weird feelings, and I didn't like it.

Someone stuck their head out and called us both in. That

didn't bode well for Lance being my half-brother. What did that even say about me? I was attracted to my brother. Maybe *all* of this was the gods punishing me for unnatural thoughts.

When I stepped inside, there were two men. My bastard father was one of them. The other was Folcard based on the crest on his chest. He was the *worst* out of all the Barons. He could be here to seal my fate because he bossed the other Barons around or...

"Which one of you is Lance?" he sneered.

"I am."

"What a disappointment. I didn't expect any son of mine to be so foppish. Must be an issue with the bitch."

Oh, thank the gods. Lance *wasn't* my brother. This changed *everything*.

I grabbed the back of Lance's shirt just in case he decided to beat the shit out of his father Guttertown style. One thing Lance and I always had in common was that our triggers were our mothers. Lance hardly ever brawled unless someone insulted his mom.

A pretty man might mean something in Folcard's world, but in Guttertown, that man could still win in a fight with anyone else in Nestran. The only one of Folcard's men I wouldn't bet against Lance in a brawl was Autar, and he didn't count. He was Guttertown born and bred.

Lance managed to keep his temper. He looked his father dead in the eye and explained exactly what I'd been thinking.

"That's not necessary. We've had both of you fall into our laps minutes apart and we're not looking for men for the military. We'll give your mother the treatment *if* you can complete a task we set out for you. You can pay us back by continuing to do it. It won't be military service this time."

I didn't like the sound of that. Not for me and not for Lance. It had been military service for the men and the brothel for the woman for decades. I didn't do well with change on a normal day. My father and Folcard throwing a wrench into how things were always done when lives were on the line and I didn't have to avoid Lance anymore?

Hated it.

"Anyway, The Ghoul and the Blight have been wreaking havoc among the people. It's given us the most delicious way to handle this," Folcard said.

I didn't think I could hate this any more than I already did, but yup, it was official.

My mood that Lance Argent wasn't my half-brother was officially ruined.

LUCY

It was so fucked up. On my walk over here, I was prepared to double down and take every precaution as one of his men so no one found out I was a woman. Why was he changing the game now? And why did it have to involve Nestran's dueling serial killers?

I wanted nothing to do with the Ghoul and I was pretty sure the Blight was either Beck or Panas since Ollie went straight to the brothel after Aimes left. I didn't want it to be either of them, but I really didn't want it to be Beck.

The Beck I'd known my entire life couldn't do that. I wasn't judging what the Blight did. Everyone he killed had it coming. If it was anyone but Beck, I'd probably shake his hand. It meant everything I knew about Beck was a lie and when I told them all my secret, he fucked me in the barn without telling me something major like that.

I'd hear Beck out, but I wouldn't turn on him. I had a feeling I was about to be put in a position where I had to choose between Beck and Mom and I hated it.

"What do you want?" Neco said.

Neco grabbed my shirt because I had a feeling he knew

Folcard pissed me off and I wanted to hit him. I knew what I looked like as a man, but he insulted Mom. I could restrain myself, but I really didn't know why he gave a shit. Or why his hand was still resting on the small of my back.

"They're both evil, obviously, but the Blight has style, and he's good. Trevils is one of the best inspectors we've ever had and he's got no clue on that one. He can't even figure out his motives. It occurred to us we could use someone like that."

What

The

Fuck.

"You want someone to kill for you?" I asked.

That was a lot. And only the Barons would hear about two men killing their subjects and choose to exploit their children when they needed help by asking them to kill for them. Why couldn't my father just be a decent man?

"Yes. We'll give you both a target."

"This is different from being a soldier," Neco said. "You can't put a knife in a man's hands and expect him to be good at it. None of the men in your employ can teach it, either. To pull off what you want requires a special skill set. I happen to have it and I have demands."

What

The

Fuck.

It wasn't Beck who was the Blight. It had been Neco the entire time. Neco made a *lot* more sense than Beck.

"You really think you're in a position to make demands?" Neco's father sneered.

"Yes, I do. Like I said, if you ask anyone else to do this, they are going to be caught. Self-preservation is pretty strong and it *will* come out that you asked them to kill for you. The people of Nestran outnumber you and the only thing between you and them are your men. If you're completely sure about *their* loyalty, by all means, don't worry about your sons. Keep in mind you're manipulating us into doing this by withholding treatment from our mothers."

Damn. Neco never really talked much but when he did, it was usually because he had something to say. It was rather badass that he wasn't afraid of his father or mine. There was a lot riding on this and Neco was brave enough to negotiate conditions.

"Proceed," Folcard said, waving his hand.

"I'm going to win your challenge. Lance won't be able to do it without getting caught. I'll be your killer, but Lance's mom gets the cure, too, and my father *never* goes near his daughter. If Momma and Rowena ever need anything further from you, you take payment from me and leave Rowena out of it. I know what I bring to the table. I also won't kill women or children."

Damn. Was this the same Neco Argent who I'd been fighting with for the last ten years? I didn't want to kill someone to save Mom. I would, but I'd probably be caught and hang for it. If Neco was the Blight, then he only killed men who hurt women and kids. That tracked with everything I knew about Neco.

He was keeping his code about not killing women or children, but he was agreeing to kill more than the guilty to save his mom. Neco also knew I would hang if I tried this, so he was giving me an out. He was protecting me just as much as he was protecting Rowena and he was making sure Mom got the cure, too.

What the fuck changed?

Folcard just smiled, and I didn't like that smile.

"Ah, but we weren't finished. We'll agree to *most* of your terms. My son needs to earn the cure. You don't get anything free in life. There are two of you. We knew one of you might not have the stomach for killing someone who didn't wrong you, so there's a second challenge," Neco's father said.

Of course. It couldn't be this easy. Neco's hand tensed on

my back and I had no idea why the warmth was comforting me. We'd hated each other for the last ten years.

"Lance can either handle the name we give him or he can take The Ghoul out of the equation."

Fuck me. Neco tried to fix it, but the only way to get the cure to Mom if that plant wasn't ready to harvest was to kill someone who was probably innocent or take on a serial killer.

Either way, I was fucked.

AFTERWORD

So, how are we doing? I hope the cliffhanger wasn't too bad. We'll get more into The Ghoul and Neco properly groveling after he finds out Lance is really Lucy in book 2, Of Thorns and Wine